Hey Pickpocket

Praise for Hey Pickpocket

It's beautifully done, rings true psychologically, as good-humored as it is deep and real.
—Neal & Betsy Delmonico, publishers, *Golden Antelope Press* and *Blazing Sapphire Press*

Is it possible to leave your old life behind and find a new one? This is the question *Hey Pickpocket* poses. Spanning cultures and continents, Allison Cundiff's debut novel restates the eternal riddle of home.
—Jeffrey Zuckerman, author of *Unglued: A Bipolar Love Story*

Guard your heart, for this book will steal it. An enchanting mix of local color, romance leavened by truth, and dashes of wit.
—Bob Mielke, author of *Calling Planet Earth*, *Adventures in Avant Pop*, and *Kirksville*

Hey Pickpocket

a novel

. . .

Allison Cundiff

JackLeg Press
www.jacklegpress.org

Cover art: Collage of a Camera Lens and Eye, CSA Images

To Brigid

What do we know but that we face
One another in this place?

—William Butler Yeats

1

...

Pickpocket. What an asshole.

If you think you got it all, think again. For one, I still have the cash I sewed into my underwear. The sketchbook, the clothes. The box of ashes.

Didn't want that, did you?

The rest is yours.

The part that gets me is not what you took, but that you put your hands on me without my knowing. I hate it when people touch others without permission. And there you were, whoever you were, reaching into my bag while I was minding my business, looking out that grimy window, waiting for the ferry.

I didn't feel you.

The thing about a thief is, you can't tell them from the next person. Same with any bad guy. They don't wear a mask or have a scar. They could be next to you at the store. They could be your kin.

Now my private things are yours. Pictures of me on a phone screen. A passport in your fingers. Your thumb rubs my name, my date of birth. In your pocket your thigh warms what you took.

Keep it.

I don't hold onto things like I used to. Anyway, there wouldn't be much of a story if you hadn't ripped me off. Funny how things work out.

2

...

If a person wanted to flee, start over, disappear, I think she'd have to be ready to leave her life behind. That's what I did.

I wanted to quit the people who knew what I'd done, find the most remote place possible, and live in the vastness of isolation. I started by getting rid of my possessions. That part—quitting my job, selling my furniture to the other shoestring-budget twenty-somethings in my apartment complex, lugging my books to the discount store, all in a weekend—was easy. There are commodities to purchase in every city and town on Earth. Walking away from the abstract familiarities of home proved harder.

My dad loved cars. He spent his time on a wooden creeper at an automotive garage around the corner from our house, legs sticking out from under the model he was fixing up. I sat in the waiting room and paged through stacks of expired magazines, listening to men discuss the Cardinals game as they stood under a car the mechanics had hoisted up. The grey shop cat slept on the counter by a corkboard wall filled with keys that rattled when the door opened.

When a customer came in, one of the men would enter from the garage and ring them up with oil-stained fingers on a cash register whose drawer would pop open with a ding when he took their check. Mom would know where Dad and I had been by the smell of gasoline in my hair. After the owner retired down south, the lot sat vacant for twenty years. Grass grew wild around it until one day someone staked a 'SOLD' sign out front and taped brown paper in the windows. The neighbors talked over their fences about what was being done with the place until the new owners posted a 'WELCOME' sign introducing a new coffee shop and offering complimentary drinks on opening day. I walked down with my mom and little brother. They'd kept the old mechanic's sign but made an adjustment: *Reliable Break Service.* The interior still had the same concrete blocks, only shined up, and the register was put on a display shelf. The corkboard and cat were long gone, as was my father, but you could still make out a seam in the sheetrock between what used to be the garage and the waiting room, and when I stepped inside, I was a child again, and I saw my father standing before me.

I made it my coffee spot. The baristas would write 'FRANCES' on my cup while I looked over the menu, though my order never changed. My favorite barista was this woman who always had a paperback sticking out of her jeans pocket. She knew my order: coffee, black, one sugar. Soon she had it ready by the time I got to the front of the line.

To disappear you have to leave the faces you see every day.

Take the woman on the train who carried a dog in her backpack. The rule was that you could bring a dog on board as long as it fit into a carry-on. I kept my distance until one day there was nowhere else to stand, so I stood next to her and winced anytime the train car jostled us. The dog's owner turned the bag around to peek at it.

"Rocky looks mean, but he's a softie."

"Oh, he's fine," I said.

"He's a rescue. He lost his upper lip in a fight. Don't worry, he's not aggressive."

After that, I stood next to her on my commute.

I was a trauma ICU nurse on nights in midtown. Disappearing from my job would have been as easy as clocking out, except for Hannah. Before every shift, for the two years she and I worked side by side, Hannah had me braid her hair. Most nurses dreaded nights, but then they had families to go home to. Nighttime kept deep sleep locked out of my life and kept bad dreams away. Can't dream if you aren't sleeping.

I would get home soon after the sun rose and crawl into bed as others were waking up. I closed the curtains, but no matter how dark I made the room, light crept in. I still heard the game show on TV next door when Donna opened her window and smoked on the fire escape. She'd tried to quit, but last Christmas she gave up, she'd told me, turning to exhale.

When you disappear, you have to be ready to let go of the people you know. You have to be willing to walk out on your life and slip into the black hole of what's coming. Force will stretch what you thought you were into a new shape, thin out your memories and your understanding of them into a singularity, your cells and your thoughts one thread.

You walk the line, brave or unfeeling.

I don't know how I did it.

I quit my job, hugged Hannah, let my little brother scavenge my possessions, and lugged the rest out into the alley for the pickers.

I bought a one-way ticket to Ireland, where my dad grew up. My mom held me a long time when she dropped me at the airport.

Neither she nor my brother asked why. They knew I was running from a dead man, whose death was my doing, whose face hung in every corner of town, the way my face hung inside the head of whoever knew the story.

3

...

Nameless in Dublin, I sprawled out under a slate sky. When I walked down Moore Street, no one looked at me twice. In a café, I told the barista my order. I didn't know my neighbors. Not a single face on the train wasn't anonymous.

On my first night, I watched a gang of girls at the corner of Cork and Patrick encircle a boy and beat him to his knees with their small white hands, as men in suits crossed the street, the kid's friends stood back and smoked, Thin Lizzy blasted from a nearby restaurant, and traffic from the Coombe jammed the intersection.

Once upon a time, Vikings traded on the Liffey. Now it divides the Northside from the Southside. Kayaks by day, lovers by night.

I waited tables in Temple Bar and waited for the Nursery and Midwifery Board to process my paperwork. The pub sulked between a mews and a refurbished dairy south of the river on Lower Bridge Street where patrons stumbled from pub to pub drinking dark beer and hollering at one another, and buskers in scarves stood on the cobbles with open guitar cases full of crumpled banknotes. The pub held jam sessions most nights as well as an Irish folktale storytelling hour. Tips flowed freely. At the end of my shift, I cashed out between the Guinness pelican and an autographed Ed Sheeran headshot.

At night I'd walk to my Northside apartment, past Pearse Street and Trinity College, now empty of the tourists who cluttered the Long Room of the Old Library or fed on spice bags on park benches. By night Trinity was a place where I could commune uninterrupted with the sixteenth-century limestone.

My otherness was invisible in Dublin.

One afternoon the leader of a group of lost girls from Chicago asked how to get to the Bad Ass Café, "where Sinead O'Connor waited tables." I pointed out the Ha'penny Bridge on her phone, and in the doorway, she told her crew I didn't seem American.

My landlady Laurie owned the bodega downstairs, Café Colmado. She loved to sit out front, and is probably sitting out front as I write this, stirring a pot of pelau, which she said her grandmother taught her to make when she was a child in Chaguanas. Dublin apartments have tiny kitchens. She carried a Weber grill and a bag of briquettes down from her balcony to the sidewalk. On my way to work, I'd see her enthroned on an upside-down milk crate, turning chicken thighs and chatting with customers amid the aroma of Scotch bonnets and brown sugar. Men with newspapers under their arms would ask how much her chicken cost, but Laurie would inform them that it wasn't for sale.

Contrary to expectation, moving thousands of miles away didn't clarify or obscure my dreams. Some nights I kept the windows open, as if street sounds would chase them away. My dead stepfather, hair matted, eyes bulging, blood down his face, stood over me.

I woke sweating, counting breaths. Laurie never asked why I left the States. I kept to myself and paid rent on time. No doubt she overheard my occasional calls to my mom through the thin walls. After a few months, she knocked on my door while I was talking to my brother. "One second, Toby," I said. "Hi, Laurie!" She handed me two pieces of mail, mistakenly delivered to her, and walked off, flip-flops slapping her heels.

The next day I stopped by her bodega.

"No macoin, I promise."

"No what?"

"I'm not eavesdropping," she said, and pointed at me with a polished fingernail. "But who do you talk to on the phone so late at night?"

"Sorry! Did I keep you up? My mom and brother live in the States."

She scrutinized my face with a complicit nod.

"Good to check in on your mama. My son should call his mother more."

I shrugged. What I took from my mother had left a gulf between us. I seldom called home.

"I thought you might have a man," she said, making change for a customer.

"No man."

"So why no man? You don't like the Irish?" She crossed the shop and stacked flats of water bottles by the cooler in back.

"I do."

"You don't like men?"

"I like them all right." Bodies on the street behind her almost touched as they drifted past Café Colmado. All the people in all the cities walked so close, they stood side by side on trains, in crosswalks, nobody saw anybody else. It wasn't going to be like that for me.

Since I arrived in Dublin I'd had two or three opportunities, but none of them stirred me much. One was Kieran, a regular at the pub, single Dad, engineer, a foot taller than me. He'd been hanging around in my section, making small talk about football. Sad eyes. His screensaver was a picture of his kids. His sister was a nurse. We talked about her until the chemistry stagnated. Another night, a fiddler named Colm held my wrist as I served him his pint. We looked into each other's eyes. He smiled, and I flinched at his soggy touch.

Local girls had it worse. One night while I was closing with Louise, who'd moved from Cork to Dublin for school, a pack showed up outside, looked in at us, and tried the door, which we'd locked after last call. Then one of them tapped his ring against the establishment's name stenciled backwards between us and them.

"Come for one more!" he bellowed, the pint sloshing in his fist.

We ignored them, talking over our mop bucket. But he went on till Louise swiveled, her face ablaze, and screamed, "Oy! That's a vintage window!"

The men booed.

"Couple of dykes!"

"I fecking might as well be, with eejits like you as my only option. Now feck off!"

Off they fecked.

I didn't know how to explain my reluctance.

"I suppose I can't tell the good ones from the bad."

It was more of a question.

"Uh-huh," Laurie agreed, getting to her feet. "You figure that out, let me know. We will make a bag of money." Her laugh trailed off behind her.

The following week, Laurie and I ran into each other in the stairwell and walked up together. She carried two bags of produce. I had takeout noodles and a bottle of Guinness. She looked me over.

"You want to eat and watch the telly?"

I gazed into the future and saw my solitary noodles and sketchbook. "Yeah, sounds great."

She pushed one of the bags into my hand, beckoning with a nod. "Here."

We sat side by side on a faux fur rug and took turns plucking dumplings out of a box with chopsticks. She flipped through the channels and settled on RTÉ News.

"How do you get news with no telly?"

"I skim newspapers in the bodega and watch TV at the pub."

"World's going to hell."

Anti-immigration protestors rammed Gardaí shields, not a mile from where we sat.

"Look at these boys."

"More like a riot."

"Let's have some of your beer then."

Laurie turned off the television. She rummaged drawers for a bottle opener. I leaned against the couch.

Loss, confined to the shadows by day, expanded to all corners of the world by night, filling the hours with its elaboration of my guilt. But who I had been didn't matter to Laurie. Only the here and now.

Takeout became our weekly date. She'd cook, and I'd bring noodles from around the corner. We painted each other's nails and talked about the lives we'd left behind. Sometimes she offered advice on love.

"Do not accept a goodnight kiss in this country, without first talk of a second date. Never go home on the first date, unless you want to. Then it is fine. Listen to how he speaks of his mother. He will treat you like he treats her. Look at who his father is. He will become his father. Every time."

She sat bent over newspaper ads to compare her price per carton of Silk Cut to those of other nearby stores. "I prefer Caribbean men," she asserted. It was unclear whether she preferred them to Irishmen, or to all others.

"Are there many here?"

"Not at all. I talk to some men on the Internet. And always I ask about their mothers."

After a few weekend meals and reruns of *Fair City,* I had become her padna, her pal. She asked me to watch her shop on my days off while she went to meet her son Anthony, who was in his second year at Trinity. Her bodega had not one cat, but five, which kept the premises free of insects, rats, and superstitious customers, ever since the day, a few months before, when a feral cat gave birth to her litter in the storeroom. Laurie put the kittens in a box next to the furnace. The night the cat went into labor, Laurie called me.

"Way seh! A rell mad scene, Frances."

"What do you mean?"

"The cat—I need your help down here."

"What's wrong?"

"She in labor, Frances. Labor! You need to help her deliver."

"I don't know about animals. I'm a nurse, not a vet."

"None ah dat!" she replied. "Get down here, girl!"

I found a YouTube video to assist with the two-hour delivery, which was mostly about making a comfortable, quiet place for the mother and watching from around the corner. Yoko, the little stray from behind the bodega, became the mother of four kittens who looked more like big mice than cats.

"A good sign. All women!" Laurie cried, lifting them while their mother licked her paws.

4

. . .

Conor the busboy looked up from a textbook propped on a stainless steel countertop, where he sat cross-legged, and asked, "What's 'terrible beauty'?" He typed on his phone. I was drying a rack of wine glasses. Mikey turned toward us from the grill, cigarette hanging from his mouth, faded Cupid tattoo illuminated in the heat lamp. "Feck if I know," he said.

"Who's the author?"

"Yeets."

Conor turned the book over. *The Collected Poems of W.B. Yeats.*

"My dad was named after him. They came from the same town." I wiped my hands on my apron and scrutinized the stern visage on the cover.

Mikey's spatula flashed among a row of burgers between us.

"Well maybe he can explain this poem. I need to have an analysis of 'Easter 1916' by tomorrow. I don't get any of it."

"He died a long time ago," I said, "or else I'd ask." A wing of chagrin swept the boy's face. I flipped to the poem. "Let me take a look."

"That line, 'A terrible beauty is born.' What the hell does that mean?"

"Which part?"

"That part. I don't get how something can be both." He poked the page, closed his eyes, and leaned against the wall.

Mikey's red face appeared in the space between the heat lamp and the counter. He set down a baked potato. "It can't. Nothing's grander than a beautiful woman."

"You can have both," I said. "If something gets too big, that's terrible. Even if it starts out as beauty."

"Like falling for someone you know is gonna break your heart," the kid said.

"Or getting scuttered when you should be stayin' home," Mikey added.

"I don't think it's about a woman."

"You two are mental, going on about homework in my kitchen," Mikey said. He leaned against the jamb and lit a cigarette. Out in the alley, snout tilted up, a dog went past at a trot.

I thumbed the worn leaves. On the inside flap, a list of handwritten names: students who'd resold the book to the campus store. All those people had held it in their hands. The author wore a dreamy scowl on the back cover. I'd stared at this photograph a hundred times. My dad hung a print of it above his dresser.

He died when I was eight. It was an accident at work. He fell off a roof he was framing.

It was nobody's fault.

I was so young when it happened, I have a hard time recalling much about him. Memories swell and burst within me. I have a handful of photographs. In my favorite, a Polaroid taken right before he left Ireland, which I've pasted into my sketchbook, he wears a bomber jacket and stands next to a beat-up Triumph Spitfire, which my mom said he used to work on back in Sligo. Another shows him in uniform: he served in the Irish Navy and was stationed in Cork. Once, while on shore leave in New York City, where the crew of the *Niamh* ate hot dogs and bought socks and magazines, he attended a Mets game at Shea Stadium. He and his shipmates hollered so loud that a woman seated nearby doused him with beer. He and Mom were married six months later.

The book's introduction described Sligo as a shelling town on a coastal plain in the northwest. I pictured my dad driving the same narrow roads Yeats walked, both their bodies moving amid crowds at the train station, coal stains on their fathers' fingers, their eyes fixed on the same river coursing through the town. Sligo was only a few hours from Dublin by train. If I went, I felt like it would mean my dad was gone, even though he'd been gone for twenty years. I looked up the population. Twenty thousand. Too big.

I turned the pages. Another poem, "The Lake Isle of Innisfree," caught my eye. Someone had circled the word "Innisfree" and written "inaccessible" in blue pen in the margin. Then a postcard slipped from between the pages and fell to the floor. I picked it up. A black-and-white photo of an elderly man's hands, with a blurry sea behind them. The palms were incised with lines. I turned it over. "An Irish Fisherman's Hands." It was addressed to a T. Archer at Corrib Village, Galway. In a feminine scribble:

> Missing you every day, son.
> Your da and I can't wait to see you this weekend.
> Let me know what you'd like to eat.
> Love you, Mum

The return address:

> Archer House, Kilronan,
> Inis Mór, Aran Islands

It was dated nine years ago. That's how long it had been since T. Archer, whose postcard this was, bought the book for a class and resold it. I flipped through the pages. The margin notes alongside the poem matched the signature inside the front cover.

I turned the postcard back over. Palms deeply lined and coarse fingers spread apart as if to cup an object, left pinky bent inward. I tried to remember my mother's handwriting. She made grocery lists on a pad on the fridge. A sloping, girlish hand. I don't recall if I ever got a letter from her.

"I'll help you with your paper," I said to Conor, "if you let me borrow this."

"Take it!" He threw the washrag. "I'm feckin' doomed." He skulked out to the dining area.

After work I walked back to the Northside and searched "Aran" on my phone. One hundred years ago, you could travel to Inis Mór, the largest of the three islands, by currach, a craft fishermen used until the Irish Republic took them out of service for capsizing too easily. Videos showed the boats tossed about, men paddling with professional urgency. You had to have fled some horrid business to hazard the turbulent, lethal North Atlantic in one of those.

Beyond the jagged Inis Mór shoreline juts a country of sunken pastureland and stone walls. The images made me lightheaded, as if I were there and wanted for company.

I texted Conor a few notes about "Easter 1916."

no worries

my roommate wrote it up for me

Really?

he did it for a pint

its grand

I'll bring the book tomorrow

naw u can keep it lol

K thanks

The island spun around in my head as I lay watching men paddle and waves break on rocks. Someone sang drunkenly below my window. I sat up to sketch the street. Lamplight streaked puddles amid an expanse of broken cobblestones. A dog barked. Two boys played stickball. The owl bus went hissing past. A busker lugged his gear. No train. No bus. Cliffs. Fields. Rocks. Population one thousand. Another millennium.

Desolation beckoned.

5

...

If the thing that hurts a woman and loves the woman it hurts is a man, then a man is not the business I'm fleeing from. If, on the other hand, what hurts a woman and doesn't love her is a man, then a man is shadowing me.

Does a thief who has robbed a woman wonder whether she is in flight, and wants to disappear, and if so, does he also wonder whether she's in flight from a man?

The man, question as to definitions, see above, whom I'm fleeing is my stepfather, Anton. Correction, was my stepfather. He's dead. My mother married him four years after my father died. They had Toby two years later. Anton and I, Mom used to say, never "took to" each other, but Toby and I did. Toby was the sweetest baby. Learning to walk he held my pinkie and looked up with huge eyes. Blond curls fell down his neck like Mom's. He's a big kid now, but he was the best little kid.

Mom put Dad's ashes in a wooden box with his name on the front. It darkened our mantel for a few years, a macabre flourish in an otherwise bright house. At Christmastime, he sat beside the tree. On the anniversary of his death, he sat on her nightstand. After a few more years, he stood on her bedroom bookshelf. Where do a dead man's ashes go? The day Anton noticed the box, I heard him and Mom talking down the hall, his voice high, hers low. He told her to "get rid of it." I put on my headphones and tried to focus on a book. I kept reading the words "the bee-loud glade" over and over.

Mom came in and asked if I would like to "keep Dad's ashes." Everything that reminded Anton of my dad had to go, she said. I said I'd be happy to "keep the ashes." She set the box on my desk and left. I stashed it in my closet next to the blanket I'd slept with when I was little.

My mother ought to have put my dead father in the earth, but she snuck him into my room like a foundling. He'd been her husband, her love. She was supposed to lay his remains to rest, not hand them off.

Adults lacked courage. If she wouldn't stick up for him, fine, but Anton wasn't going to say a word to me about my father.

The problem was, I didn't know where my dad wanted to be scattered.

I remembered the nights when the three of us walked down to Romano's, where they'd sit and talk past my bedtime, and he'd order wine and they'd eat pizza and I'd color until the crayons were worn down. I dozed with my head on his lap, and his belly rumbled in my dreams.

Yeah, I thought, I'll bury him in a midwestern strip mall parking lot.

He worked on cars and collected car magazines. He listened to ball games on the radio. He'd gone fishing with his father after church on Lough Talt. His mudders looked gigantic under his side of the bed, compared to my sneakers. The seatbelt in his car felt snug and smooth against my chest.

Not much else remains.

His voice, with its accent, went first. Sometimes he would show us home movies of his family's farm in the north of Sligo. Cloudy sky, slow sheep. It was always raining where he was from. His talk of the old country died with him.

The ache went next. After a few years, the absence that had felt like a hole in my chest turned into the knowledge that grief had been my last connection to him. Then that shrank into a speck, numb and sempiternal, at which point I grasped that he was gone.

Shards turn up now and then. When I see a man the age he would be now, with the same stride, I wonder. I assume his posture, as when he slung his left arm over the back of a chair to sit at the table. I see his fingers around a bottle of beer at the end of the day, a ring of condensation left on the table when he lifted it to his lips. He took his tea black with sugar, the way I take my coffee.

Years later I would trot out pictures, black-and-whites of his parents, who'd struggled to conceive, his Mom told me, and had my dad in their forties. He was so unlike them, he joked about being adopted. They were conservative Catholics, very observant, and their "feral cat" joined the Navy and served as an ensign, later lieutenant commander, on the patrol vessel *Niamh*, so named after the daughter of a Celtic sea god. After his discharge, he moved to the United States and worked as a carpenter. In one photo he brandishes a hammer and grins through a mouthful of nails.

One time I asked my mom to set up the projector, but she winced as if the very mention of him thrust a splinter against her insides. I grasped this eventually. My father, the person to whom she would have turned in her grief, had fallen from a ladder and died instantly, thus without ritual, let alone a valediction forbidding mourning.

What guide, pickpocket, could she have invoked to direct her steps?

Was it a comfort that my father died a painless death, as the coroner informed her? Was it supposed to be a comfort? Was his death without fear? That's more to the point: a plunge, the foot on the rung slips, not an emotion but horror, my stomach sinks at the image of it. His nonexistence got under my skin. He was thirty-two, the age I'd be in a few years. Sometimes his daughter looked so much like him that his widow shuddered at the sight.

I mentioned him less and less, but I still sat cross-legged on my bedroom floor with the box of ashes.

I asked the box if it wanted to be scattered at Westhampton, where my father and I waited for our bobbers to dip, or beneath the tree he parked his truck under so we could climb. I asked whether I should wait until Mom died, and ask her box.

Not even the box in my head said a word in reply. No help was forthcoming; from whom would it come? I kept myself to myself, and I stashed the box in my closet. I complained to it about my stepdad, and boasted to it about testing into Freshman Honors Science class and winning the nursing school's Science Ambassador scholarship.

He was a good listener, in death as in life.

When I left for college, I wrapped it with flannel and packed it in a milk crate next to my iPad and sneakers. Thence from a dorm room closet, where he sat for a year, to an apartment closet. I had a boyfriend who started staying over long enough to keep some clothes at my place. We would do our homework together, taking turns flipping the record. One night, after a particularly unremarkable session of lovemaking, he jumped out of bed and rummaged the closet for a sweatshirt while I opened two beers from the fridge.

"What's in the box?" he said down the hall, scratching his chest.

"My dad." I handed him the bottle.

He stared back at me as if I'd told him a dirty secret.

"Ashes? Like of a dead person?"

We weren't together for too long after that. As I like to say, one Missouri winter was all it took for the romance to cool.

I still have the box. It occupied the windowsill of my room in Dublin, then my backpack, then the Aran Islands.

I'll play my part and bring him back to where he was born, but it's the last part of him I possess, and I'm not inclined to part with it.

Sometimes we aren't ready to let things go, even if they hurt us, especially if the hurt is all we have left of them.

Everything that reminded Anton of my dad had to go.

With one exception.

When Anton looked at me, he saw his widowed bride's late husband.

Anton is dead, too, pickpocket. That was my doing. Those ashes, she got rid of. No one would want them hanging around.

Anton's death resulted from a traumatic brain injury. Not all TBIs are fatal. His was. The impact caused substantial internal bleeding, in addition to the external bleeding that left a stain on

Mom's floor. Six months later, a worker applied a solution to the living room carpet to lift out the spot.

Out of all the systems I studied in nursing school, the brain mystified me the most. It had no quick fix, unlike other organs, and the way people talked about it felt clinically ambiguous. The brain fascinated neurologists, but different parts of our anatomy attracted me. Women's health! Superior reproductive capacity. The human female incubates her young for nine months and survives. No wonder the ancients sculpted images of fertile bodies swelling with new life.

Or the heart, that working-class organ.

The rush of pressure was what thrilled me. I thrived on that chaos.

Emergency medicine was my business. My job was to save lives.

Not take them.

In Anton's case, the TBI was caused by blunt force trauma to his parietal region, the part of the neurocranium that protects the left lobe of the brain. Which it did not do when I struck him. The blow likely caused an interference between the nerve fibers, which led to inflammation, followed by fatal axonal injury.

I didn't mean to kill him. I hit him with a garden pot. I tell myself I had to. He was strangling my little brother. Toby's face had turned red, his eyes glassy. An obstructed airway can cause brain damage in under three minutes.

Mom tried to pull her spouse off their son.

I went to the mudroom, picked up a garden pot, carried it into the living room, and dropped it on Anton's head.

6

...

I thought I could go back. Same coffee, same night shift, same big sister, same face, same name. If someone were to ask whether you'd kill to save a life, you'd say, "Sure." We amble around inside our certitude as if it were a continual Now, with no feel or inkling of what we'll think later. But smashing a skull scathes you.

It's been two years.

I went to work, I was a big sister. But the memory struck back at me. Standing in line at the grocery store behind a man who raised his voice into the phone. Sitting in a theater watching a movie character flip out.

The light that streamed across Toby's face, his swollen eyes, the thunk of the pot, the crimson thread. Did my hand raise the pot? My arm swing down?

The spirit scar healed tight and pink.

The currach. Unused, remember, since World War II. I asked the boy at the Galway ferry station counter about the currach. He scrutinized my face.

"No, ma'am," he replied. "No one uses those anymore." At a desk behind him, an old man, soggy cigar stub in his jaws, squinted at me over a newspaper.

"Just curious!" I perused the brochure.

The first ferry departed for the largest of the three islands, Inis Mór, at 9:40 am the next day.

"Is this the earliest time?" I asked. The boy was counting euros, thinking with his lips.

"For. That. Commercial. Yes. Unless. You. Want. To. Go. Over. On. A. Private. Boat."

"Private boat?"

"Fisherman's boat," he paused his tally. "They carry locals back and forth. Ten quid but you'll be standing the whole way."

The commercial boat was twice the cost, and so—and also since I had a postcard with a fisherman's hands on it (which I've mentioned, and about which more later)—I bought a ticket for the fisherman's ferry, whose queue prior to the 5:50 am boarding time the next day, comprised a pair of wind-scarred fishermen, an old woman in a kerchief, and lastly myself, with the hood of my sweatshirt up against the predawn rain.

ONE WAY: KILRONAN HARBOR, PAS BORDALA.

I think a thief would have to be in sad shape to rob a girl fleeing for her life, or is it from her life? But I guess you slid your fingers into my bag because you didn't figure me for a crusher of men's skulls, did you, pickpocket darling. No one else thinks of that when they look at me, so why would you? Woman, backpack, invisible. I bet you wouldn't have ripped me off if you knew I slept with a baseball bat, a sure sign I don't play.

When you sleep with a bat, people let you be.

I know something you don't know.

In the cramped cabin I watched dawn spread across the gelid surface astern of us. We sailed away from the Ros a' Mhíl Terminal, turned south through Baia di Cashla, and crossed the mouth of Galway Bay. Waves stretched between the vessel and Connemara. With sunrise on our port side, the frigid North Atlantic looked orange to starboard. A few months ago I'd dropped my coat in the Liffey where it empties into Dublin Bay, and reached in to fish it out. Icy for sure. But downright sizzling if you compare it to an adult of my species with eyes full of hate.

When I told Laurie about Inis Mór, she didn't ask why I would travel to a place with fewer than a thousand residents. She insisted, however, on sewing a money pocket into my jeans on our last night together, sitting barefoot on a stool in my room as she hummed over her needle.

"Keep your money hidden. The pros clean out your pants and your coat with one bump." They'd be miles away, she said, before I knew I'd been robbed.

"I'm going to miss you."

"You're a hard worker," she laughed, curls bouncing as she gazed up, needle suspended in space. "Don't forget to play."

"Guys?"

"Pleasure. Happiness. Joy. You can stay in my spare room at Christmas. We women have to stick together." She thrust a lacquered fingernail at me. "There isn't one good man in this whole town."

"Says the woman who tells me I need a shag."

"There's shagging," she smiled, "and then there's loving. Just keep your wits about you." She stood and presented me with the jeans.

I slipped them on, the new inside pocket against my belly.

I left by train that evening, promising to keep Laurie updated; spoke with the ferry terminal clerk, see above; and checked in at a hostel on Quay Street. The other two women in the room snored so loud I couldn't sleep, so I checked out, walked to the ferry station, and waited for dawn, when I boarded the boat that was about to transport me to the land of the unseen.

On deck, I grasped the rail, shrugged on my backpack, rewrote a text in my head to send to Laurie (*All good, early boat, so cold!*), then reached for my—

Empty pocket.

I rummaged the backpack. The purse, passport, and makeup bag were gone. That left my father's ashes, wrapped in a few articles of clothing, and a sketchbook.

There were four of us on board, plus a captain who chatted with the men in work clothes. I'd followed them across the platform and onto the boat, and memorized the backs of their heads. You and I must have touched for just a moment, as we stood in line waiting to board different vessels. And now I was alone.

7

...

I huddled against the exterior of the cabin, sheltered from the wind. Squinted at the scud, the choppy surf, the wake, an empty bucket stenciled in Gaelic rolling around on the afterdeck, the ferry terminal cup of coffee asway in my guts.

I staggered toward the bucket, turned it over, and sat, head on knees, sucking air. When I glanced up, two men were peering out at me. One spoke to the other. The elder of the two stood in the doorway, moving his lips, saying something, evidently to me. A gale tore the words from between us, his; also a few errant teardrops, not his. The red skullcap hovered stiffly closer, the pale brow furrowed.

"You all right, miss?"

"Dizzy, I guess."

"Seasick."

Amid the gray bluster I saw my father's face as he bent down over a trembling stranger on their jaunt across the Acheron.

The second man, wearing the same cap and stowaway jacket, his face younger but with the first man's sloping forehead and light eyes, leaned out of the cabin, peering in the direction we'd sailed from, then met my gaze with a distant observance, before turning away.

The ferry lurched into the trough of a wave whose crest cast a shadow over her. Spray streaked the windows. My stomach sloshed. I shut my eyes. If I went over, the fishermen wouldn't find anything but a box of ashes. But they'd be dry.

I took a deep breath and pictured the Russian steppe, black earth stretching as far as the eye could see. Also a small fire.

A calloused hand offered me a thermos. I drank from it. My hand trembled as I screwed the cap shut.

The younger one was about my age. "Thank you," I said. "I haven't been on a boat in forever."

"No trouble at all. We're almost there, and the rain's about to clear off." He sized me up. "It helps if you look in the direction you're headed." He pointed to a misty landmass.

I stepped back inside and rested my forehead on the glass as the horizon came into focus. I stood on tiptoe, shaky, and saw slate crags loom and a jetty thrust into the bay. Swells lapped pylons slick with algae. A man in a glass box on the dock directed traffic, a thin parka whipping his belly. Tidy houses and stone fences peppered the coast, a vibrant green between them.

The vast grey sky was a salve. Something unspooled in my chest as the boat slowed down. I pushed hair from my face and handed the thermos back to the older man.

"Thanks very much."

He nodded with an easy smile as the boat jolted to a stop.

"There's tea in that pub," he said, pointing at a stone house up the hill.

The captain knelt and lashed the boat to a cleat on the dock. A sign that read 'KILRONAN' blew in the wind. The younger fisherman held the starboard gunwale to steady the boat, his hands broad against the wooden rail. Beyond him on the pier, a squad of fishermen lingered, faces turned toward the mist.

The other three passengers moved toward the exit with the somnolence of habit. I disembarked last. Stone walls divided plots of land in haphazard pieces like fingers at the end of an outstretched hand, clutching at steep hills. I lifted my bag, shielding my eyes and feeling a thousand departed islanders watch me arrive.

A cold welcome for the murderess.

I considered the hillside path to the pub, which wound past horses grazing in the mist. Men dotted the harbor beneath white gulls swooping in noisy arcs. An old woman in a plaid shawl hobbled toward the row of houses. The two fishermen walked off in the other direction.

I had no direction, no number, no name.

I had a postcard.

8

...

The two fishermen walked off into the sodden wind up the pebbly road toward a cluster of buildings. I drew my rain-soaked coat around me and trailed them alongside boats whose crews watched me pass, big creels of fish with oily, bulging eyes stacked at their boots.

In the brush under the pub's thatched eaves, beside a tremendous cat, heedless and recumbent, lay a sign reading 'BOGHADAIR'S.' The men entered through a creaking half door whose top was guyed off by a frayed rope slithering in the wind. Smoke ebbed from the chimney. A young man crossed the road, donkey in tow.

Through the front window I saw the two men standing beside a large hearth where a woman in a colorful sweatshirt gestured to them. I pushed through after them, a bell heralding my entrance. At a workbench, a richly bearded man in a leather apron glanced up at me through thick glasses. The men I was following had removed their caps and set their sacks down. The younger one passed a hand across his eyes, as if to wipe the ocean from his memory. The woman handed them platefuls of bread and noticed me with a nod. I walked past copper pots hanging next to the stove and a black dutch oven on a slab in front of the fire, where tangled bunches of dried heather hung. Against the wall by the open window, a selection of items for sale: lures, fishing line, leather gloves, hand balm, army knives, long underwear, and used hardbound books, half in Gaelic, half in English.

"Welcome," the woman said. "Can I help yah?" I turned around. She pushed up her sleeves.

"Hello," I said.

"Oh dear, you're drenched," she said, and came to my side of the counter.

"Yes, sorry." I looked around for a phone.

"No trouble at all." She led me to the shelves. "We don't have macs, but we have these." She nodded toward a stack of wool sweaters in cream, taupe, ivory, and tan. "They're fishermen's sweaters."

"Macs?"

"Raincoats."

"How about an umbrella?"

The two men chuckled. I wiped hair from my face.

"A sweater will keep the rain out better than a mac," the younger one said. "An umbrella won't do you any good out here." He pursed his lips above a steaming cup of tea, his thick fingers black around the nail. I glanced directly at his face for the first time. It was chapped, with a rugged brow and a fair complexion, like mine except for the pale eyes and closely cropped chestnut hair. We looked away from each other.

I'd begun to warm up.

"It will turn inside out in the wind," the older man said.

"Sweaters work just as well," the woman said. She took one off the stack and unfolded it. "The general store down the road will have a mac, if that's what you want. Do you know your way around yet?"

"I just got here," I said. I tugged the straps of my soaked bag back onto my shoulder.

"Welcome to Inis Mór." The sweep of her arm told me that wherever I stood, I'd be standing on the whole island at once.

"Where do you come from?" asked the bearded man at the bench.

"Dublin," I said. "I heard they have rooms for rent in town. Do you know where I could look?"

"This *is* the town," the woman said. "Several good places to stay right along our main road."

"Could I borrow your phone?"

I'll call the embassy, I thought. No, I'll call Laurie. No, I'll call, I didn't know.

"Mine was stolen in Galway."

The younger fisherman shook his head with a low whistle, and the same lines appeared on his brow as on the older man's. Father and son.

"Stolen?" the woman asked. She must have been the wife and mother. "Where did you last see it?"

The kindness of a bystander's questions about a lost thing always implicates the person who lost it, as if being helpless weren't enough, as if to lose something were to be irresponsible.

"At the station, I think," I said.

"The three of us were on the early ferry over from Galway," the older man said.

"That port is full of crooks," the younger man said. The bearded man nodded. I pulled my coat tight around me. "Come by the fire," the woman said, and took a yellow telephone out from under the counter. It had a cradle and receiver, the sort of model a housewife would gossip on in an old movie, coiling the cord around her finger. I did as I was told, like a shivering child.

"Wanda has rooms for rent. She's a fair price, and she's right behind us," the woman said. She pointed to a laminated map of the island. The names and legend were in Gaelic. "This little store is us, and there's a pub on the other side."

I squinted.

"No tourists till summer," the woman said, "so Wanda will have space. You can walk on over. She'll look after you." She pointed to a door that led to the pub.

"Thank you," I said. "I'm sorry about the mess."

"Dear, we're a fishing island. The floor can handle it."

I sat on a stool beside a brick arch and stared into the turf fire. The nausea had passed. I'd never seen such a big fireplace. At my back a group of islanders chattered.

"Something to warm you so," a voice behind me said. I turned and saw the bearded man, offering me a cup of tea.

"Thanks," I said, but he'd gone back to his bench. I took a long sip.

There was only one way ahead. Either back the way I'd come, or forward. Wind blew hard out there beyond the streaming windowpanes. To make it this far was not nothing.

Forward it was then.

I walked over to the sweaters and lifted one from the pile. It was made for a man, broad in the shoulder with cables up the front. A second was larger, with a crisscrossing rope pattern. I held the fabric up to my face and breathed the scent of lanolin.

"Are these made locally?" I asked.

"Those were," the woman said. "The ones we carry are knitted by hand. On the mainland, they'd be from the factories." She helped the older fisherman into his coat.

"See you this afternoon, love," the man said, and kissed her forehead and moved toward the door. The younger man averted his eyes, pulled his hat on, and followed the other man out, his cheek reddening.

"That's my husband and eldest son," the woman said. "They didn't move off island like my brothers, so I get to see them every day."

"Your husband is kind. He gave me some water on the ferry when I got seasick."

"Sounds like you had a rough morning," she said. "You American?"

"Yes. I've been in Dublin for work."

"Welcome to Inis Mór…"

"…Frances."

"Maude."

We shook hands.

"That there's Declan," she said, pointing at the bearded man.

"Hi," I said. He nodded and smiled. "Tea was lovely. Thanks again. It's your shop?"

"Aye," Maude said. "My shop and pub."

"There's something about this sweater," I said. I'd seen Aran sweaters, but these felt earthen somehow. I'd never heard that they wicked moisture off the body. The men had seemed warm in theirs. I liked the way the younger man's sweater hung on him.

He was tall and lean, built like someone who worked outdoors all day, his physique shaped by labor. I pictured the layout of the young man's anatomy as his mother stood before me.

Maude lit a cigarette. "Each sweater has its own design to identify the one wearing it. Long ago, fishermen would sometimes fall overboard due to wind or rough waves. It would take a day or two to find them, and by then it was too late. Only the sweater would be left to identify him." She made the sign of the cross with her cigarette.

I looked at the ropes woven across the breast of the sweater. An embedded architecture. In the States it would be a costume, or something you'd wear if you lived on the coast. Maybe if I moved to the Eastern Seaboard or the Pacific Northwest, I would take up with a coastal man. Decent. An island type. He'd wake up in the morning and put his fisherman's sweater on.

I watched a woman walk past the window with several young boys in tow, dressed in trousers and oversized mudders. Miniature men. I imagined Toby growing up in a place like this.

"Our Aran men are raised to be skilled fishermen. They aren't afraid of the sea; they respect it. Our island depends upon it."

"Do they take their children with them? To fish?"

"Many do," she said. "My husband brought Tom Junior with him."

His name was Tom.

"Declan here is our cook."

"Pastry chef, ma," Declan said, looking up over the glasses on the end of his nose. "My specialty is tarts," he added. He looked about my age.

"Do you fish as well?" I asked.

"I'm a creature of land," he said.

"Declan here is a master in the kitchen," Maude said. "Tommy's the sailor."

"He might know the waters, but don't let Tommy near a stove," Declan said. "He'll ruin a perfectly good leg of lamb."

"Not a chef, God love him," Maude laughed. "But the fish, they fall into Tommy's lap."

"Poems too," Declan said.

"Aye," Maude nodded.

A poet fisherman, if you please. A make-believe man.

I looked back at the sweaters and touched a cardigan.

"That's the Tree of Life pattern," Maude said. She pointed to another. "That's a Flaherty pattern. The Flahertys live on the north end of the island. Only ones up that way. Another family of fishermen. You know, some islanders say the Atlantic is our biggest ally. It has always defended us."

"Against whom?" I asked. I ran my fingers over the woolen knots.

"Invaders. But that doesn't mean water doesn't have its problems. It can be cruel."

"Cruel?"

"To islanders. Especially during the stormy seasons. It keeps us isolated. From supplies, from medicine. It's claimed many lives." She stubbed out her cigarette in an ashtray. "Hundreds of years ago, they say, fewer fishermen could swim. Now they all can, but then, not so much. Their boots and clothes weighed them down, and fathers used to tell their sons they'd be more careful on deck if they couldn't swim. They'd better respect the sea! Of course, things have changed. All the Irish on this island, the first thing we do with our children is teach them to swim."

I wondered whether mothers here worried about the water. I remembered swimming lessons on cold Saturday mornings at the Y. I hated the pool. On the final day, we had to line up at the diving board and jump into our instructor's arms below. I remember the woman treading water smiling up at me, her outstretched arms and flotation device. I jumped, but just once. I was a land person. Did the mother outside with her three boys feel like she was surrounded by natural forces hungry for her young?

If I were an Aran mother, I thought, I'd lead my child down to the shore, even if it was cold. I'd teach him to swim in the waves, I'd take his face in my hands and make him promise to swim like hell if he fell in.

9
...

I chose the one with the chain stitch and chestnut buttons. At the counter, Maude lifted it with a smile.

"These patterns were kept guarded for years," she said. "Used to be only family members could wear them. People nowadays aren't as protective as we used to be."

"Do you know this family?"

"Of course, dear. This is our sweater. Our name is Archer."

Missing you every day, son.
Archer House, Kilronan,
Inis Mór, Aran Islands

I shivered. These were the people. Were these the people? Those must have been Tom Junior's annotations on the "Lake Isle of Innisfree."

"Are you, I mean, do you mind if I wear an Archer sweater? If it's not my name, I mean."

"No problem at all," she said. "Seldom happens, though. Seems like you could use something warm. I'm happy to have you wear one of ours." She punched buttons on the register.

"May I use your restroom?"

She pointed through the pub door, where a young man stacked logs by a lighted fireplace and an old man shook open a newspaper. I latched the door, took the postcard from my bag, reread Maude's note to Tom, and slipped it back into the book. I looked at myself in the mirror, missing you, for the first time since I'd arrived, hearing voices, every day, from the pub's patrons through the Archer House wall, Kilronan, Inis Mór, Aran Islands, missing you every day, son. Hair plastered to my forehead, color drained from my cheeks, I looked like the wreck of the fair vessel *Frances*. I splashed my face with water and tied my hair into a stubby ponytail. I unbuttoned my jeans, drew a wad of euros out of the pouch—while actually saying aloud, "Thank you, Laurie"—unfolded a soggy €100 note, crossed the pub to the shop, and bought the sweater and a tube of lip balm. Maude counted out my change.

"I texted Wanda. She has two rooms available. The view is pleasant if you don't mind the sound."

"Sound?"

"Of the tide," she said. "And be warned, Wanda's a talker."

"Does the room include meals?"

"It does. Breakfast after your overnight will be here, but we have dinners too, not included. Regardless, you should come for a pint this evening once you're settled. My treat."

"I'm making brown bread," said Declan.

I nodded. Maude handed me my change. I thought of the boats, the cliffs, the way Tom's long silent body exited the store.

My rival in secrecy, Inis Mór.

10

...

Dense mist clogged the air. I dodged puddles past a row of trestle tables that led to a thatched house at whose mossy entrance the rotund Wanda, clad in a tight apron, swept her stone stoop. The eyebrows above her ruddy face shot up when she saw me.

"Frances, yeah? I'm Wanda. You're soaking wet."

"It rained on the ferry over," I said, and shook her pudgy hand.

She smiled. "I'll show you my rooms. Twenty euros a night for the smaller one. That includes your breakfast from Maude's there."

"Sounds great," I said. We ducked inside. Two children busy with crayons and cartoons ignored us as we took a passage to an outbuilding, older and colder than the house, without much iron or wood. Wanda unlocked the first door on the hall with an ancient key on a chain around her waist.

The diffuse gleam of midmorning lent a somber cast to the close space of the little room. It had a double bed, a fireplace next to a stack of wood, a kitchenette and toilet, and two east-facing windows with views of the sea. Wanda drew the drapes and said it was drafty, and I'd hear boats and kids. She asked how long I planned to stay. I told her a few weeks. She raised her eyebrows.

Beams crisscrossed overhead. Explosive surf thrummed through the stone blocks and shook the domicile as foamy waves tumbled landward. Ships crept along the horizon. On a table under the windows stood a stack of hand-painted mugs and a kettle.

A spot for Dad.

"I have another room in back that's warmer," Wanda said. "It's twenty-three euros a night."

"I'll take this one."

"You'll have to make your own fire. Gas boiler doesn't reach."
She propped the broom in the fireplace corner.

"That's okay." I'd never built a fire in my life.

"Suit yourself."

I filled out the paperwork in Wanda's kitchen and gave her a week's rent up front instead of a passport. She showed me to a telephone in the hall where I could call the embassy.

"You're welcome to one of our cell phones, since yours was taken," Wanda said. "The kids have them too." She nodded toward four enormous blue eyes, gazing up from the rug.

"You can borrow mine," said the boy. His chubby hand offered me an oily, smudged device. "Hers is only 3G."

"That's nice of you," I said, "but I don't mind not having one."

"Grand," he said, "cause I play a lot of Genshin Impact."

"So, what part of America are you from?" Wanda folded her burly arms across her bosom.

"Midwest," I said. "My father was from Sligo."

"So you have Irish in you then. What do you do for work?"

"I've been waiting tables since I got to Dublin. But I'm a nurse."

"A nurse!" She clapped her hands. "I suppose you've got stories." My cheeks flushed.

"Not many pubs here, I'm afraid. Hope you aren't looking for Grafton Street."

"I'm looking for something slower."

"You've found it," Wanda said. "Not much craic here, compared to Dublin."

"Sounds great," I said.

"If you want more than a week, you should stay on." She lowered her voice and glanced from side to side in mock confidence. "Our doctor is always overwhelmed."

"Only one?"

"Aye. Dr. Neuth. Her clinic is up the way." She pointed out the west window toward the center of the island. "She's had an ad out for help. It's been two or three years."

"Years?"

"Not many people want island work. No nightlife, no shopping." She clucked. "Maude has maps. I'll text her."

I asked myself if I was the only person on Earth who felt like being alive was being invisible.

Wanda proffered a room key. "There's just the one," she said. "So…"

Declan and Maude walked in, bearing a menu and a map.

"Any recommendations for sightseeing?" I asked my hosts.

"Dún Aonghasa is where most people go first," Declan said. He leaned his elbows on Wanda's counter. His hair, beard, and fingernails were trimmed and clean. A finely groomed man. A fastidious version of his brother.

"You churchgoing?"

This was Maude. She sketched a squiggly map of the island's sights on the menu.

"Christ, Ma, you can't just ask someone if they're churchgoing," Declan said. Wanda snorted.

"It's for the ruins," protested Maude. Declan doodled a Celtic cross.

"I love a good ruin," I said.

"Enda's buried there," Maude said. She tapped a central spot with the pencil. "Facing the east."

"Who's Enda?"

"Irish saint," she said.

"Irish ghost, more like," said Declan. "You'd best watch yourself." His longish black hair was greying at the temples.

I bent down over the map. "Ghost?"

"Dinner's on me," Declan said. "You skipped our breakfast."

"Thank you," I said.

"I'll tell you some ghost stories," he said. "Four until close."

I watched them cross the street, Declan's arm around his mother. He held the door and they went in.

In the hall I left Laurie a voicemail reading out the address of my lodgings and saying her pouch was a lifesaver. Back in the chilly room with its bare walls and whitewashed quilt I laid out my things on the table: clothes, books, Dad. I draped the clothes over chairs and wiped the windows with my palm until the vast grey coast came into view, waves rolling under moorings and docks, wind shaping the shore.

I turned the box this way and that under the shadeless light, and considered the density of ash.

To what base uses we may return.

"Did you visit Inis Mór?" I asked.

The box sat silent. As ever.

At the mirror, I peeled the clothing off my cold limbs. Naked in grey-blue light, my frame looked silvery. I held the sweater against my chest. I slipped it on. The fabric scratched at first, then felt warm. Dad built fires when it snowed, and his turtleneck stank of smoke. I sat at the window watching fishing boats, white dots, guessing which one I should choose, *that one right there*, to be the boat that Tom was on.

11

...

A small dog with filthy fur and a bent ear sat panting at my door that afternoon when I stepped out into the fog.

"Hey pup."

I'd lain down and dreamt. A scenario entitled *The Second Worst Night of my Life* was now entering year two of its run on the big screen in my brain.

Anton hovers, closing in. Blood in my throat, I watch his fingers squeeze Toby's neck. The arms won't budge, no matter how hard I haul on them. Anton turns to face me and leers. Blood leaks from his wound. Is it fiction? Is it real? I try to back away, but my legs are too heavy, I try to scream, but I have no mouth. I know I won't make it, but I have to try, even if it's too late. It's too late. And then I wake up and spent half an hour under the quilt in a cold sweat, trying to chase the dream from my head by reading the guidebook Laurie gave me when I first arrived in Dublin, the one she'd used years earlier as a newcomer from Trinidad, which only devoted two pages to the Aran Islands and touted Dún Aonghasa, the prehistoric stone fort Declan had noted, as "a must-see destination" three miles from where I lay.

I headed west, toward the cliffs. The dog skittered off but caught up after a mile or so, hopping from stone to stone, pausing when I turned to look at him, ears flapping, paw poised.

"Come," I called, patting my thigh.

He cocked his head. My childhood pet beagle, TickTack, came no matter who called, and bayed at every living thing in sight, but this one backed off when I approached.

I followed the curved road, consulting Maude's map, the dog trailing me at a distance.

I passed an establishment called Watty's, in whose window calligraphic letters advertised 'TRADITIONAL MUSIC.' Two women sat outside drinking tea from polished cups. Turning right, I could make out Na Beanna Beola, described by the guidebook as "a series of wind-scrubbed summits beyond the mist across Galway Bay."

That mist was turning to drizzle. A herd of sheep huddled in the vastness, spots on a sward. Stone fence work interlaced this coast, splitting the land into homesteads. Dún Eochla, "one of the highest points of the island, affording a spectacular, nearly 360-degree view," hovered in the far atmosphere. Stone rings stood at the center of an unpaved path, encircled by bands of tall grass, disheveled by the wind, changeless for thousands of years.

I marveled at forts that shielded islanders standing watch over the sea, alerting their people to threats. Ghost women hitching up their skirts to scramble over stones gazed at me out of prehistory.

Three girls pedaled past, shouting back and forth. A colony of gulls in the wind shrieked about a colony of seals on the rocks.

The dog shadowed me alongside roofless walls with loose stones in their doorways and farms where women wearing headscarves hung clothes out on lines and cows grazed. An old man wearing a suit jacket, oxfords, and dress socks mounted a squeaky bicycle and coasted downhill in a puff of pipe smoke.

Lighthouse. Sentinel of oblivion.

Stone by wet stone, clear to the top. I turned all the way around. Grass. Fences. The Atlantic.

The dog whimpered. I leaned down and looked into his watery black pupils.

By midafternoon, I'd reached Dún Aonghasa. Rows of jagged stones ringed the fort. A walkway led from the road to the edge. Beyond a gray horizon.

The fort was built more than three thousand years ago, in the Bronze and Iron Ages, the guidebook said. From here, the Medieval Irish looked out for enemy ships, massive, slow antagonists.

The limestone was what as the poet said. A terrible beauty.

If you fell to the talus, there would be no chance of saving you. No stable C spine. Major head trauma. Broken pelvis, widespread ecchymosis. It would be three seconds of terror, and a brief, bright pain.

The dog whined.

I had banknotes sewn in my underwear and a wooden box of ashes.

"Since the 1500s, the Aran Islands have been a place of pilgrimage, offering refuge to holy men and women. St. Endas brought Christianity to the Aran Islands, training the devout who built monasteries."

I sat and sketched the landscape. Then I drew a pair of hands placing a stone block. Then waves breaking. Tom Junior's hands on the ferry gunwale. Tom Senior's hands holding a cup of tea.

The dog inched toward me. I pulled a piece of jerky from my pack and offered it to him. He sniffed the air. His nose twitched. Then, head down, he took it, his eyes on mine. He backed away and chewed.

He panted and was silent.

12

...

Back in Kilronan, I crossed paths with patrons ambling two by two toward the pub. Maude and Wanda leaned against the wall and waved.

"Michael Collins!" Maude cried. "He's been gone since Wednesday. Where did you find him?"

"Michael Collins?"

"He's an Irish dog."

"He was outside my door this morning. He followed me to Dún Aonghasa and back."

"He's Tommy's," Wanda said. "Goes out on the boat with him."

"Tom'll be happy you brought him home," Maude said.

The dog scurried out from behind me. He hurried past her, scratched the back door open, and disappeared.

"You walked all the way to the west side of the island?" Wanda asked.

"I did," I said. "It was beautiful."

The women looked at each other. Maude stubbed out her cigarette on the wall.

"The embassy called," Wanda said. "I left their number next to the phone. Will you join us for a pint?"

"Thank you," I said. "Just have to change. I'll be right over."

In my room, I took inventory. Every article of clothing I'd brought would fit in a single drawer. My mother had stuffed a cotton dress into my bag that I'd worn waiting tables. I combed my hair and smoothed out the damp wrinkled thing against my body, and whichever way I turned, I had a windblown look, outwardly my inward self, I supposed. I slipped the sweater back on. If the doctor needed help, then maybe I would help the doctor. My stomach rumbled. Do we want to be ballast tethered to another person, I wondered, do we want to carry them?

What kind of weight was I?

In the mirror I stared at the little line between my eyes, visible in my dad's forehead in old photos. Fair skin and dark hair.

His image, this heritage.

13

...

Framed photographs, portraits of no one famous, hung unevenly on mahogany walls around the entrance of Maude's dimly lit pub. Under a large Irish flag tacked on the ceiling, the clientèle sat and stood, silhouetted against late afternoon light descending on gulls in the road. A man with a round head framed by tufts of white hair leaned against the bar and guffawed. Another holding a suitcase smoked at an open window under a 'NO SMOKING' sign. Wanda spoke to a young priest with slick hair, her two children playing cards beside her, Michael Collins at their feet.

Across an interior the size of a living room, Maude poured tea for a man in oilskins while Tom Junior, all suspenders and saturated wool, chewed an unlit pipe in a corner booth. His eyes settled on me. How do you enter a pub without imitating someone entering a pub? I made my way to the bar where Declan, ignoring his tea, frowned over a pair of ramekins.

"You made it!" he said. "Help me choose a tartar. One of these has too much lemon. You picky about mackerel?"

"No one's ever asked. On any other day, I might be."

He pushed the dishes toward me. I took a bite from each and pointed at the piece of fish to my left.

"This one."

"Me too."

"It's fancy. Sweeter."

"Dill. Can you believe it?"

"You must be very experienced."

"Thank you, Miss Frances," he said. Then, "Dip that in there. It's clarified butter."

"I could drink this," I said, chewing.

"Practically a seasoning on our little island," he said. "It does make our coffee drinkable, though."

Declan's smile posed the question of what sort of man Toby would grow into, now that he no longer dwelt in the sunrise of boyhood, but had stepped out into daylight, still a skinny kid with giant hands and feet. Would he be good? I hoped I'd still like him.

Maude materialized at my side and pulled me by the sleeve. "Everyone!" she called out.

The music stopped. Two dozen patrons turned our way.

"Everyone, this is Frances. She's from America."

Maude put an arm around my shoulders, as if to introduce the new kid to a cafeteria full of drunken classmates.

"And she's just brought our Michael Collins back to us!"

"Hiya, Frances," said the multitude. Some nodded, some raised their pints. I felt Tom Junior's eyes on me. I looked at him as he sipped his beer, then looked away.

"You found Michael Collins?" Declan said. "Where?"

"Outside my door. He just stuck around."

"Hero," he said.

"Come sit with us," Maude said, and gripped my elbow. "We're by the fire."

I smiled politely at Declan and passed faces that turned to look until we reached Tom's booth.

Clad in heavy canvas dungarees and a bloodstained thermal, curious amusement in his eyes, Tom resembled Declan in pigment and build, except that he was weary from labor, hence less manicured. He stood to greet us and looked me up and down. In his father, and in the old sailors nodding off beneath the television, I saw what Tom would become. The hands on the postcard.

He smiled, stood, and sat in the opposite seat.

"What'll you have?" he asked.

I slid into the booth, a marlin on his line.

"Oh, nothing for me," I said.

"You brought old Michael Collins back."

As he spoke he held a fist in front of his mouth to cover crooked teeth. His cleanshaven throat sloped smoothly from chin to shirt collar, pink from a day outdoors. How would it feel to touch his Adam's apple?

"Least I can do is buy you a pint."

"Okay. I'll have what you're having."

Tom nodded and rose. I considered his height, the broad shoulders, the tapered chest. That shape had been his work. He moved to the bar, not efficiently, with the smooth precise hands of a doctor or nurse, but powerfully, with strong thighs, crossing the room as if it were the deck of a boat. Wrinkles covered the back of his shirt, untucked below a line of sweat down the spine.

My belly felt what my eyes saw. How long had it been since a man's mere looks threw me off my center, how long since I couldn't cool the heat flooding my limbs like a liquid fire?

Liquid fire, get a grip, for fuck's sake.

As Tom talked to Declan, an older man with a heavy mustache leaned in, and the conversation swallowed them. Declan saw me looking and smiled.

"So, you went to Dún Aonghasa, did ya?" Maude asked. Wanda pulled up a chair.

"I did. I'm waiting on the embassy, and I have a little time on my hands. It was first on my list of sights to see."

"Windy one, yeah?" Wanda said.

"I'm glad to be by this fire."

"So Michael Collins tagged along?" Maude asked.

"A few feet behind me the whole way. I gave him a bit of my lunch as thanks." Both women laughed.

"That's several miles on foot," Wanda said.

"My plan tomorrow is to visit the clinic."

"Are you hurt?" Maude asked.

"Not at all. I'm a nurse. Wanda thought the doctor might want help."

"A nurse!" Maude exclaimed. "Tommy," she shouted. He turned toward her. "She's a nurse!"

Tom caught my eye and gave his mother a nod, his cheeks coloring.

"You came all the way from America to be an island nurse?" Maude asked, and sipped her tea.

I nodded.

"You aren't going to talk to me about my smoking, are you?"

"I might," I said. "It's especially hard on women, you know."

"I'm going to quit after Christmas," Maude said. Wanda raised her eyebrows. "Anyway, Brigid could use the help. The last assistant she had was, how long ago?"

"Five years, I'd say," said Wanda.

"Five years," Maude said. "We had some islanders study medicine, but they all stayed on the mainland. My Tommy was at university himself a few years back as well." Tom placed a pint in front of me. "But he prefers to stay close to his mum, don't you, dear?"

"This is true," he said, back in the booth. He drank and wiped the foam from his lip with the back of his hand.

Tom's cerulean eyes scanned mine. He was unreadable. If wind and water metamorphosed into a man, it would be him. A girlfriend of mine had once gone on an Alaskan cruise and brought back a calendar filled with photos of loggers and sled masters that looked like him. A lonely woman's fiction. I didn't care if he turned out to be pulp romance personified. I could have stared at his feral face all day. I imagined those hands that held the hull holding my hips instead.

"You all right then?" Maude asked.

"For sure," I said. "What did you study at uni?"

"Earth Sciences. I can talk for days about rocks."

The pub's heavy door creaked open, and Maude and Wanda leaned back to observe the group of men who entered, wearing the same uniform, with the same long workday in their bodies.

"Let's check on Declan," said Maude. "Orders gonna be coming in." She and Wanda went to the bar, smiling at the priest, the pub's most distinguished customer.

"Thanks for the pint," I said.

I never made small talk outside the hospital. I asked patients to tell me about their pain, tell me what they needed.

"No trouble at all," he said, rubbing his shoulder. "Let's see. You're an American nurse, here on holiday to help locate lost animals."

"Right," I said, "but not exactly on holiday. Might stick around for more than the weekend."

"Where did you find my dog?"

"He found me. He was outside my door."

His eyes narrowed. "Doing what?"

"Sitting there."

"Just sitting there, so?"

"He didn't offer any more information."

"Did you feed him?"

"When we got to the cliffs."

Michael Collins' white snout poked up at me from under the table.

"You've bewitched him," Tom said.

I scratched the dog's head.

"I've never been to America. What's New York like?"

"Everyone asks about New York. Why not Missouri?"

"Where's Missouri?"

"Below Chicago."

"Sound. We're behind the mainland. Plenty of tourists come through, though."

"We don't have those. But this pub looks like it's full of locals."

"Not the season quite yet."

"I understand why people come here. What I've seen so far is beautiful."

"Has its perks, if you like remote." Didn't he wonder why I'd cast myself adrift here? "You'll stay with Wanda then?"

"That's the plan for now," I said.

He leaned back and saw me glance at the sunburn on his neck. "I know," he said. "Sun cream, right?"

"Nurses notice these things." What was his skin tone where it wasn't burnt? "The boats I passed today were big. Do fishermen live on them?"

"I stay there half the time. But I have a room down the way, on Fishermen's Row. It's a line of single-room apartments for blokes like me."

A pang that wasn't hunger made me nod.

"Right by the pier. Keeps us close to work. Just a set of stone houses that share walls. I can hear my mates snoring after their dinner, for fuck's sake."

"No kidding," I said. My leg bounced under the table.

"Anyway," he said, "not much room for craic when you're up before the sun."

"Sounds like honest work. It's good for you."

"Guinness is good for you," he said, lifting his glass. I lifted mine. "You having another?"

"I'm good," I told him, my head swimming. "Declan told me I should try his bread."

"Right. I'll get it. Or else you'll wait forever."

Tom headed toward the kitchen. I reached for my—

—empty pocket. Neighbors smoked pipes by the open door. Two young women, barely of drinking age, sipped and chatted, their faces inches apart. One watched Tom go round the bar: Tom as the islanders saw him, a village fixture, property of the village, belonging to a village girl. A man in a porkpie hat and thick boots sat down beside the hearth as though he were settling in for the night.

Dublin equaled celibacy. What about Inis Mór?

Tom came back with a loaf of bread wrapped in wax paper and two bowls of soup. Declan, flour in his beard, followed with a dish of butter. "How could you forget?" he said.

"Right," Tom said. He broke the loaf in two and spread the butter on one half.

"Jesus, it's grand," Tom said, dipping bread in the soup. "You're a feckin' genius."

If Laurie were here, she'd ask Declan what he used for his stock. Then she'd ask Tom what he thought of me.

Declan nodded. "Tom has been my taster since we were wee lads."

"He owes me," Tom said. "He wasn't always so skillful."

"Who's older?" I asked.

"Ha!" Tom said.

"You can't tell?" Declan asked.

I looked from one to the other. They stared.

"I'm older," Tom said, slurping soup.

"Look at how the age hangs on his face," Declan said, "He's thirty!" He walked back through the pub's swelling crowd.

"Irish twins, not fourteen months apart," Tom said. "Try it."

I brought a spoonful to my lips. Julienne carrots and lamb cubes. He reached across and smeared butter on my half of the bread.

"How many tourists come here in a year?"

"Loads. But I haven't seen anyone as lovely as you take the worker's ferry and nearly pass out. You're in health services. Couldn't you give yourself something for seasickness?"

Couldn't I give myself something for butterflies?

"Sadly, dimenhydrinate doesn't affect existential dread."

"What's that?"

"Dramamine." I swallowed another mouthful of soup. "Motion sickness medicine. Do you ever get seasick?"

"Used to it by now. Why the dread?"

I heard a twang and turned to see the men by the fire lift instruments from cases on the floor, two violins and a mandolin. A woman dragged a chair over, and they formed a circle.

"Losing my passport and phone, traveling by water."

"The water's a friend. But I understand. It's unpredictable."

"Do you like what you do?"

The music started.

"I was born to do it."

I sat too far to hear his voice as clearly as I wanted. Too far to see him. Smell him. Touch his skin.

Now four men and one woman sat facing each other, each with an instrument on their lap: two violins, a mandolin, an accordion, and a flute. The man with the mustache who'd been talking to Tom dragged a stool over to the circle and drew a tin whistle from his pocket.

"Have you seen a seisiún before?"

"Traditional music?"

He nodded. The audience hushed. Declan switched off the TV. The woman put her hair in a ponytail and tuned her violin. They nodded in unison and played the first chord. The fiddler leaned in. The woman lilted, the sweet tone of the first bright note bursting softly in the air. Tom stared, his long body still.

"This is called 'He Moved Through the Fair.' It's like a poem."

My eyes lingered on his face. What would my dumbstruck Missouri self, my nonchalant Dublin self, say about this sight? I listened and drank.

The music began in a minor key. The woman sang a story about a poor young couple longing to marry. The musicians accompanied her, as she assured her lover she could convince her father that money mattered less than love.

> *"And he went his way homeward, with one star awake,*
> *As the swans in the evening move over the lake."*

Yeats' wild swans: "But now they drift on the still water, / Mysterious, beautiful." The singer looked as if she were the girl in the song, in love with the boy, giving up safety for love's sake. The rest of the bar was silent as old and young gazed toward the music. Declan stood behind the counter, his arms crossed, a dishrag over his shoulder. At the end the violin trailed off together with the woman's voice, and everyone applauded. The musicians drank, then began to play a reel.

"See that in Dublin?" Tom asked.

"Not quite."

"You like it?"

"Yes. It's a poem. Like you said."

"I've known that song since I was a kid. Those lyrics! Impossible love."

"Impossible?"

"How she loves him? Despite them being poor."

"I don't think that's impossible."

"Suppose it depends."

"On what?"

"The quality of the love."

The group modulated into another key and began a new song.

"An old rebel tune," Tom said. An older couple clapped in time. Declan led Maude to the dance floor. Tom Senior cheered.

"Anyhow, sorry about your personals. Did you get it worked out at Wanda's? Embassy and all?"

"I did. It'll be a few weeks before I can go anywhere. They're mailing me a replacement from the States."

"That's not so bad."

"Not bad at all."

"I have to ask. Was the water I gave you this morning what cured you?"

"From a medical standpoint, yes, I was probably dehydrated."

"And Maude's sweater?"

"You were right. Better than a raincoat."

"Looks nice on you." He appraised the sweater's contents.

Declan, Maude, and Wanda came over, out of breath.

"Well, I'm beat," Wanda said to Maude.

"Stay for one more," Maude said to Wanda.

"I would, but I have the room to get ready." She turned to me. "I'll get your fire started for you, Frances. It gets cold here after dark. G'night everyone!" She went out the front door, raising her coat against a late spring rain.

"You didn't get a fire going?" Tom asked.

"I've never lit a fireplace before," I said. "Is there central heat?"

"Not in every house," Declan said, nudging Tom. "Wanda's is an older build. All stone. You're likely to freeze."

"One of the boys will show you," Maude said. "It would be good for you to learn."

"That would be great," I said, and thought of Tom in my room, seeing my things.

Declan and Maude discussed the next day's menu. Michael Collins stretched out in front of the table. Our shadows lengthened in the firelight, our faces aglow.

14
...

I woke to muted light, my head adrift from the stout. The last embers had turned to ash, and I could see my breath. Boat engines. I tucked my hands under my armpits. When had I last been touched? Not since I left the States, yes, but when exactly, it must not have been memorable, how long ago? I ran my fingers along my abdomen and thighs and inhaled the scent of tobacco in my hair. If you looked from the left, you could see a streak of motor oil down Tom's neck. I ran a bath for him in the tub in my head, and smoothed a washcloth down his sunburn. Hands pressed the small of my back. Fingers dug in. My thoughts were wet. My breath came quickly.

No one knows what I know.

Including me.

I sat up in bed. I hadn't dreamt. Yesterday had chased the bad dream away, I supposed. I stood on the cold floor and spaced out, watching morning bathe the boats with steep sun as they bobbed at their moorings in the harbor.

Is every little island an open secret? The upside of stumbling through life is that there's a chance you'll land on an Inis Mór. Pastry chefs, spotty internet, fishermen. An Old World fantasy whose inhabitants were not, thank you Yeats, terrible. If it was too good to be true, I was okay with that. No one, including me, knew what I knew.

I'd sat in the booth with Tom and Declan till last call, Maude's eyes pausing when she noticed our heads still bent in conversation. For an endless final hour, Tom and Declan had asked about nursing, starting with the question everyone always asks. I never know what y'all want to hear. By *worst* do you mean saddest? The kid in the trauma ICU next to the drunk who ran over his bike? Do you mean the most unlikely object lodged in a rectum? Are you asking me what threats we've received? Unless everybody in the booth is wearing scrubs, I keep my mouth shut.

"What kind of 'worst thing' do you want to hear about?"

"Like something you'd see on a telly drama."

"My saddest case was a young father, early thirties, a police officer wounded in the line of duty, intubated, likely brain-dead."

"What happened to him?"

"Not sure. But every afternoon his wife and son filled the windows in his room with handmade posters that said 'GET WELL SOON DADDY.'"

"That's adorable."

"Yeah, except his dad wasn't going to get better."

"Jesus."

"The son signed each poster *Sinseer, Beau* next to a stick figure of his father in uniform."

"Fucking 'ell."

"Yeah."

What I didn't say, one of the things I didn't say, a single one of the many things I didn't say, was that sometimes surviving traumatic injuries is worse than dying from them. I heard the thwack of the TBI that I'd personally caused, and I lingered in perverse pleasure a moment, then snapped the memory shut.

Pickpocket, I sometimes wish you'd filched a memory or two.

Tom stared the whole time I was speaking. Suddenly, as if he'd sensed my discomfort, he asked if TV shows depicted medicine as it was. Not really, I said, grateful to him for changing the subject, signaling to him that I was grateful, seeing him see the signal, seeing him show me he'd seen it.

They displayed their injuries, bearing their sins before a priest of pain. Declan's thick scar from a kitchen knife. Tom's from a rope that had cut through him. Another of Tom's, this one on his flank. He lifted his shirt to show a wedge of torso I'd picture the next morning. I spotted yet another cicatrice across Tom's lip. He seemed to be covered with them.

The lower the beer sank in his glass, the closer his face drew to mine. He talked about life on the boat: sunburns, puncture wounds from hooks, bruising from rough water, a friend lost to the drink, concussions. Tom had never traveled farther away from home than England. Declan had attended culinary school in France, where he'd fallen in love with a pastry chef named Daniel.

"Where is he now?"

"12th arrondissement, in a one-bedroom apartment barely big enough for the both of us." I imagined two men trying to cook around each other in a Parisian kitchen. Declan leaned in closer. "He comes through every now and again. Brings his own Le Creuset. Superstitious about his cassoulet."

Tom said, "I don't understand one word of that."

Two brothers, one disheveled, the other coiffed. Disappearance had never been a possibility. As soon as I was here, I was known. Were they suspicious?

They asked about you, pickpocket. I described Laurie's pouch. They were amazed I wasn't angrier. I could have told them I was, but what for? They didn't ask the only relevant question. I would have lied, of course, although I believe they could have understood. Some chapters are better left unpublished.

Maude turned up the lights. We stood. Declan embraced me.

"Thanks for coming to dinner."

"The best I've had since I moved here. Maybe ever."

Tom said he'd see me home, all fifteen feet across the soppy road to Wanda's.

"Dark out," he said, holding the pub door. We exited into a cool, clear night. Hands deep in his pockets, he stopped as I unlocked the door to the room.

"Night then!" he said, and turned away.

"Night!"

He rounded the corner.

I latched the door and warmed my hands at the fire Wanda had made. I sat for a long while watching flames consume the wood she said Tom and Declan had chopped the week before. The events of the day flashed like film stills.

I showered and left my mother a voicemail with my new temporary address. I wrote Toby a postcard saying the fishing boats lined the shore, the pebbles reflected moonlight, and the sun set on the sea. I said he should visit soon, not that our mother could afford to send him. I said I loved him more than all the world and sketched the view from my window below the signature.

What I'd told Toby was true. My heart belonged, and belongs, to my little brother. I don't care who his father was.

Footsteps, then a knock. Toweling my hair and dressed in a t-shirt, I opened the door, and there beside Michael Collins stood not Wanda, but Tom, with my bag in his hand.

"Oh," I said.

"Morning, er, afternoon."

"Afternoon."

"You just up?"

"Had some unpacking to do last night."

He scanned the room over my shoulder. I eyed the bag in his hand.

A North Atlantic chill invaded the narrow passage.

"You left this."

"Thank you."

The sketchbook and guidebook were still there. I pulled the blanket around myself.

"Don't you have work?"

"It's Saturday."

He doffed his cap. I petted Michael Collins.

"You're all wet. Would you like me to light your fire?" He leaned on the jamb. His eyes were bluer by day. "We don't want you to catch pneumonia."

"The bacterial infection caused by wet hair?"

"It's a matter of public safety."

"In that case, come in."

To the list of things a man should do to stir my interest—ask me a good question or two, press his palm against my lower back (see above), write me a letter by hand—I now added: build a fire. I'd watched men kindle campfires as a child, but I saw the act anew as Tom bent to inspect the flue.

"This one looks good, though Wanda should have given it a good cleaning out before she made your fire last night. Not many tourists through the winter." He lifted split logs from a basket on the hearth, a long match between his teeth, and stacked them tightly above the ash while Michael Collins sniffed in the corner.

I sat on the chair between Tom and my dad.

"When does the tourist season pick up?"

"Soon. Me da and I figured that was maybe what you were here for, when we saw you on the ferry over."

Tom sat on his heels, the orange light on his brow. We watched the little blaze.

"See how I did it?"

"Sort of. Very old-fashioned."

"Old is better built. Next time it's your turn. I'll talk you through. You'll freeze if you can't make a fire. Even in summer." He appraised my bare legs and wiped his hands. I stood. He was a head taller.

"Thanks for returning my bag."

"No trouble at all."

"Did you look inside?"

"Is that where you keep your secrets?"

He turned to the fire. Wanda's television droned from the main room down the hall. For as long as I could remember, I'd watched the male of the species mask his fear with antics—schoolboy rituals, insults, insinuations, aggression, contempt—and whether it was the cattle call of social life or an appointment with an older professor whose lechery I had to earn, I didn't find much relief. By contrast, at least so far, Tom either spoke as if I were a friend or flirted with me, and either way, his regard felt open, brave.

"You coming to eat?" he asked from the door. "Declan made pain au chocolat."

"Traditional Irish breakfast?"

He laughed into his fist.

"How do you eat Declan's cooking and stay in such good shape?"

"We're all in recovery from the Great Hunger."

"Thanks for the fire."

"See you in a bit, so."

His step receded through Wanda's door into the afternoon wind.

I sat and watched the firelight spread. If he looked in the sketchbook, he'd know I'd been watching him. Which might not be so bad.

It seemed there was no pub meal without fanfare. Declan, his eyeglasses fogged with steam from the teapot, floated among the tables with powdered sugar and fresh fruit while Maude added wood to the fire. I winced my way through a cup of her coffee and skimmed the *Irish Independent* for news of Dublin budgets and Dublin crime. A few men watched soccer. Fishermen discussed Friday's catch, which was still in the cooler on the boat, to be unloaded later that day, when there was less wind. Maude topped off my coffee and asked if I wanted cream or sugar.

"Just sugar."

"Not black?" Declan asked.

"I like sweet better."

"You and me both."

Tom walked out from the back and stepped into a pair of mudders.

"Watch that fire at Wanda's," he said to me, and pulled his cap down. "There's rain expected later."

Maude looked at Tom, then at me. Declan smiled. She swatted his arm with a dish towel.

"How's the coffee?" Declan asked. "Never had it black with sugar."

"Want to try?"

"I will yeah!"

"Does that mean no?"

"'I will yeah' means definitely not," Maude said.

"We are strictly a tea family. Try this then," he said, tipping in a finger of Baileys.

I considered the oily swirl. "Is this how you take your tea?"

"I'm a teetotaler."

"Good for you."

"Being sober in these parts is more scandalous than being a full-on homosexual. I should know!"

Maude laughed. "Declan hasn't had a drink in how many years?"

"Seven years this December. Not good for the figure." He patted his stomach. "But despite it, I never judge a man's drink. Unless it's coffee."

"I saw lots of straight-edges in the pub in Dublin, regulars who would come in to play music and have tea."

"Aye. The pub is more about being social," Maude said.

"But seriously, Miss Two Sugars, any more details about the fire at Wanda's?"

"What's that?" Tom asked, walking up alongside us.

"The, uh, fire," I said. "Any special instructions?" I avoided Declan's gaze.

"Keep the flue open. Keep your personals away," Tom said, lifting suspenders onto his shoulders. "Even if you catch the cottage on fire, you'll be all right. It's stone."

Declan bit into a pastry and grinned at his brother.

"You said you were going to help me here today," Maude said.

"We're unloading yesterday's catch. Back in an hour, Ma."

"What are your plans today, Frances?" Maude asked. "More cliff-gazing with Michael Collins?"

"I have a job interview."

"Feck off!" said Declan. "That's grand!"

15

...

News of the Irish citizen from America seeking employment as a nurse had already reached the island doctor, who left word at Wanda's that I should drop by. Maude sold me a €1 map and I rented a bike from the corner shop. I laced my boots while Wanda prattled about the leaky clinic roof and her son Padraig played kitchen chemistry TikToks by an American he was sure I knew personally.

Wanda scrawled *hill past McAulay's farm, second left by church* on a receipt, and I cycled north through warm mist along stretches of farmland divided into rundales. By the time I reached the worn MᶜAULAY sign, the map was pulp on the handlebars. A donkey meandered toward the fence through a chicken flock; I patted her nose and gave her an apple from my backpack. The higher I rode, the further the island unfolded below, although my angle of vision concealed the cliffs. A farmer lumbered around his property, leading a cow by the halter and carrying a bucketful of greens. The animals parted for him, and he took his time, hand on their bony spines. Horse herds shook manes and swung tails, lifting soft heads. Women rambled across uneven dooryards. I bore left, up to a one-story building whose sign read 'OSPIDÉAL.'

Dr. Brigid Neuth shook my hand firmly in both of hers. She was my mother's age and had comely features and tired eyes. File cabinets lined one wall of her little clinic, curtains and cots the other. Behind the counter serving as a reception desk, cases of Fanta lay piled next to a stack of last year's magazines with the name *Seamus Mullen* on the address label. I followed as she fussed about. First, she asked how much clinical experience I had, then how I'd handle an angry patient who didn't want to wait for an appointment, then what my rotation in obstetrics was, and what specialties I worked in. She listed her needs: treat the injured, digitize paper records, and travel to the mainland and other islands for supplies and treatments. She'd need emergency help, but my hours would be standard, Monday through Friday, on-call on the weekend.

"I hear you're Irish, so?"

"Half. My father was from County Sligo."

"Brilliant. I've been desperate for someone the past year, especially during the tourist season."

"When's that?"

"It's quickly approaching. We're already beyond capacity as of last week." She wrapped an elastic band around her hair. "Cliffdivers with concussions and infected cuts. A woman in labor who required transport to the mainland but delivered en route in midair, a boy, nine and a half pounds."

"That's a big boy," I said, and pictured myself having a baby in the sky.

"I've been up to ninety this whole season by myself."

"I'd love to help, Dr. Neuth."

"Brigid. I was named after the church on this island. Have you been?"

"Not yet."

"Right, so you'll start Monday then?"

A gunshot wound broke up the going-away party that my colleagues at my last hospital threw for me in the nurses' station, and when the day shift crew arrived to scavenge the leftover cake, we resumed the festivities in a pub around the corner, a dimly lit establishment in the Garden District with a wooden bar and a framed photo of Michael Collins. It was eight in the morning, and we ate hamburgers and told Kenny, our favorite bartender, what had happened, while he shook his head.

Exiting the clinic I spotted a beach and steered off the coastal road onto a gravel trail through the grass. Children splashed while a man in a scarf watched them. Crabs crept across the film of algae on the rocks. I parked and walked to the water's edge. Distant boats shimmered. I slipped off my shoes and stepped in.

16

...

Rain fell that night and the next four days. The storm swept the village and rattled the windowpanes of a solitary room where I sat in bed and beheld the blurry harbor—small boats covered with canvas tarps at anchor, large craft on the horizon—added wood to the fire, and reread Yeats or sketched the day's views. At times I thought I ought to feel lonelier with only myself for company, but I couldn't summon up the sorrow, and dwelt in whatever this was, instead.

That Tuesday I had my first patient, a toddler with fever. She tested positive for strep, and when I tried to administer the amoxicillin, she shut her lips and eyes, so I poured a little tea onto a sugar cube, and put the spoon in my mouth, then repeated the gesture with medicine on a sugar cube for her. She acquiesced to her mother's applause.

That night I called Laurie. She'd rented my old place to an opera singer and added a clause to the lease stipulating no scales past 11:00 pm. She also told me she'd started dating a Trinity instructor.

"Did you meet his father?"

"Long dead, Frances. I can't rely on my tricks this time." She had a good feeling. He'd taken her on a private tour of The Old Library after hours.

"That's romantic."

"I'd ask about fun for you, but not much of that in a small space, right?"

"Not yet."

"Good Lord, I can hear the rain."

"I've been stuck reading by the fire."

"You sound like an old granny woman. Leave it to me, girl. I'll have fun for the both of us."

"I'll live through you."

"You stay dry on that little island."

Two days later, a large, dented package arrived from Laurie containing my last paycheck from the pub, lip balm, a sketchbook, and two chocolate oranges. I'd decided against a cell phone for now, though Brigid said I'd need one.

On the second evening of rain I leaned against the window watching two men in baseball caps drive their traps down the road. Rain fell in long, grey streams, collecting in muddy puddles. The fire in Wanda's hearth crackled, and her kids splashed in their bath. I called my mother.

"Frances!"

How was my rented room? Was I warm enough? What was the clinic like? Was I eating healthy? Was I sleeping?

"I can hear Toby bouncing his basketball."

"He's grown two inches in four months. He misses you."

What to say? Hey kid, sorry I murdered your father, miss you too!

"I miss him too. How's he feeling about high school?"

"Can't wait. He's trying out for basketball."

"I'm sure they'll take him."

"Do you like it there? The small town and all?"

"It's peaceful."

"Let's talk at least on the weekends? You're getting a new phone, right?"

"It's kind of nice not having one."

"I'm going to get lunch started."

"Call me on this number if you need anything, Mom."

"I love you, honey."

"Love you too."

My first week on Inis Mór, Tom went to sea twice, two days each voyage, and on both occasions, time expanded or contracted according to my thoughts of him. I'd caught glimpses since that first night in the pub, but nothing more. I kept turning corners, hoping to see him. One day Tom Senior showed me which slip his own boat was tied in, and said Tom Junior's would be tied in the next one over. From then on I could tell from my window whether he was on land. What were the nights like? What did he think about?

Talking with Maude over breakfast, I searched her face for traces of Tom's. He had her fair eyes, her skin, her gestures, her way of resting her head in her hands when she listened to someone speak. Above the register stood a framed photo of a little boy, dressed in suspenders and a child-sized Aran sweater, with dark tousled hair, a sunburned nose, and a smile missing two teeth.

"Is that Tom?"

Maude stiffened. "No one's mentioned my Seán yet?"

"No."

"That's my youngest son."

"Handsome guy."

"He was. He's gone now, though. He drowned when he was six. The tide took him. I don't get many opportunities to talk about him."

"Beautiful photo."

"Tommy took it."

"They resemble each other."

"Seán was a surprise. I was in my forties."

"Happens all the time."

"Well, I was sure it was gonna be a girl. He felt different. I wasn't sick for a single day, and I carried high. Tommy and Declan carried low, as boys do. Seán was born right here in our bedroom. Another boy. I couldn't have been happier."

"A home birth. You're strong."

"All three boys were born right here."

"Did Brigid deliver them all?"

"Two of the three. Tom Junior came before she could get here. His father presided. You might say he's been an admirer of the medical profession ever since. Seán would have turned sixteen this year."

She put down her dishrag and sat on the cooler across from me. I laid a hand on her forearm, and she laid a hand on mine.

"That, my dear, is the big heartbreak on the island."

It made sense Tom would stay here instead of Galway. "I'd like to hear about Séan when you're inclined."

Maude smiled softly, her eyes scanning my face.

I swallowed hard. "I lost my dad right after I turned eight."

"So young." She lit a cigarette.

"My mother became a quieter person."

"Aye. But you remember something of him?"

"I do. He was Irish, actually. From Sligo. Served in the Irish Navy before he moved to the U.S."

"Good man."

"He loved working on cars. Always wore coveralls, stained by his work."

"That's grand. How did you settle on our island if you have people in Sligo?"

"I just wanted somewhere quiet."

"Have you been to County Sligo yet?"

"Not yet. I want to get settled, then take a trip. I don't have any family left there, but I'd like to see where he grew up."

"Beautiful county, Sligo. It's hard with the dead. People don't know how to talk about it."

"We can talk sometime, if you want."

Maude leaned on the bar. We stayed that way for a while.

17

...

Now villagers approached me, first with nods and smiles, then with quips about the "dirty sky" or the "cutting wind" that brought them in for a pint, then with requests for advice about sundry ailments they sometimes seemed to have kept bottled up forever, which I fulfilled as best I could.

A woman at the pub, who'd been married to Brigid's cousin for fifty years and had grown weary of her husband's way of blowing on his tea, asked in confidence whether I offered marital counseling. At the clinic young women furtively solicited suitable birth control methods, and rather than recommend abstinence, my technique of choice, I reassured them that our conversation was confidential. Talked them through the family planning brochure. I advised two men to wear sunscreen, and an elderly woman named Birdie to have an X-ray taken for her knee pain, which meant a ferry ride to the mainland. I told a man Tom's age, who'd just opened Inis Mór's first beef farm with his four sisters, and squinted over the pub menu, too embarrassed to ask someone to read it to him, that he should stop by for an eye exam, and a week after the visit he came back wearing new glasses and carrying two churns, one for me and one for Brigid, both of which we gave to Maude. Every last islander wished to know, first, whether I was married, and second, how many children I planned to have once I "chose a chap."

The succession of days brought about a peculiar inversion in my experience of time. Every conversation I had was aboveboard. I stored the daily details in my head rather than in texts and posts, and after work I sat at my window reading, sketching the coast, and listening to the Galway radio station.

My first week in clinic we treated, then had airlifted to Galway, a boy gored by a goat. Brigid got him to admit he'd tried to ride it on a dare. The American nurse from Missouri earned the approval of two Texans diagnosed with dehydration caused by stomach flu. Brigid closely monitored the pregnancy of a young ballet instructor, who taught a handful of schoolgirls while seated on a foldout chair in her garage dance studio, dressed in tights and ballet slippers—not pointe shoes, which Brigid forbade—the impending arrival of whose baby the islanders awaited like a celebrity or a storm.

Brigid asked why I'd chosen to work at her clinic when I could make "loads more" on the mainland, and she seemed to understand when I told her the same thing I told everyone: I wanted a place with fewer people. I told her my long-way-home bike rides to Maude's had become a ritual, I was sleeping better, the pub's patrons had welcomed me. Brigid herself had stayed on, after all.

If no patients kept us late, and we closed promptly at five o'clock, I took a trip to the cliffs. Islanders didn't go cliff gazing, but the tourist season hadn't arrived, and I could bike there and imagine that the wind was urging me onward like the gentle breath of a kind god. The cliffs offered the sweetest of my new pleasures—sea, sky, and gulls—and canceled out everything that grieved me.

But often, after a day's work caring for the wounded and ill, my body sank between what had been and what was to come, and the horrid scene played out over and over, as distinct and present now as on the night it took place: the unvarying dream of Anton's grabbing, twisting hands, his thick forearms, the living room at that same hour of night, a blurry beam in the ceiling coming into focus as I woke sweaty and shaken and sat up to peer out at the twinkling dock. What was I doing, thinking I could hide in the Atlantic night?

At bedtime I read to Wanda's kids out of books the ferry delivered to borrowers on Wednesdays from the University of Galway library. If we ran out of material in the meantime, I had recourse to Jack, who lent out books from his fudge shop: a paperback entitled *All About An Bradán Feasa* portrayed Finn, the man who ate a Salmon of Knowledge, and their favorite, a detailed account of Bram Stoker's origins that featured a vampiric creature known as The Abhartach.

In my sketchbook I pasted the photos I'd taken with a Polaroid camera from a secondhand shop: Declan at his workbench, Michael Collins on the pier, Tom Junior laughing behind the bar, Brigid digging in the community garden behind the clinic, whose topsoil Tom Junior had mixed according to his own recipe, with seaweed, sand, and donkey manure courtesy of Birdie.

After dinner I paced up and down in my room, glaring at an empty boat slip; cycled around the island; and haunted the pub, where Maude leaned back next to Seán's photo and dragged on a cigarette. All without variation, until—at nine o'clock on the third night of my third week, when Tom had been in Galway for two days—Declan dropped by Wanda's.

"How ya getting on, Frances?"

I stirred my leftovers as Wanda played Candy Crush. "Just grand."

"Oh no," he said, looking at my cold noodles, "not that for dinner!" He shook his head, took my hand, and led me to the door.

"What's wrong?"

"In France, the way you cook, and the way you eat, reflects your mood, your future, everything. You're going to imitate the French from now on. It's Pork Pie Time."

"What does that mean?" I put on my sweater.

"You'll see."

I followed him into the pub, past a group of men playing cards, and into the kitchen, where he switched on a mixer and blended eggs, butter, and flour.

"I promise you this will be worth your time."

He poured kombucha into two coffee cups and handed one to me.

"Where'd you get this?"

"Tom brings it from Galway." He took a sip and sized me up. "So, what do you think of our little island?"

"The pace is slow. People mind their own business."

"Do they now?"

"If I could relive my life, I'd live it here. A little stone house, a little yard with a goat and a cow."

"I suppose the many downsides haven't come to your attention?"

"I'm all ears."

He faced me with the gravity of a barrister.

"Did ya know the priest once doubled as our undertaker?"

"Souls by day and bodies by night!"

"They used to hold the cadavers in this very building. Right on the spot where we stand."

"Are you trying to spook me?"

"Are you spooked?"

"The living scare me, not the dead."

"You're in good company then. Our little paradise is fulla ghosts. This pub used to hold stiffs from all over the island before their burials. My parents bought it off the last owner, not caring a damn we could have all been haunted. Wild if you think about it. Though, since you're a nurse, I'm sure you're used to death."

I assured him I was.

He lifted the dough from the mixer and rolled it out on the cutting board.

"So, eh, divorced?"

"No."

"You have someone?"

"No."

"Single?

I nodded. "You?"

"There isn't an eligible man anywhere on the island. Plus these parts aren't friendly to the unconventional."

"Has it been hard for you here?"

"Varies from person to person. Sometimes I feel like a proper outcast, if I'm being honest. Is it any better for my likes where you're from?"

"St. Louis had a little Castro Street. They called it 'The Grove.' If you go to the city, any city really, you'll find a diverse community."

"Diverse, how?"

"Gay, straight, black, white. There was even a small Native American population."

"Like Chief Joseph?"

"In school I sat next to this guy in Literature class named Dylan White Antelope."

"No joke?"

"He moved there from a Reservation in the second grade. We always sat next to each other because we had the same last name. He was a member of the Osage tribe."

"Were you sweethearts, like?"

"Not at all. We were in school together forever, but we didn't talk until ninth grade. He stood out, but he didn't care. That's what I loved about him."

"Stood out how?"

"He missed a lot of class for rituals. His Dad would pick him up and take him out for the day. I was jealous he got to leave, and I wondered if he had a choice to participate in ceremonies, and what it was like for him when he went."

"Nice guy?"

"Yeah. Quiet. But not withdrawn. Stocky like his Dad. Good at writing poems. Recited one at the talent show freshman year."

"Tommy was good with those sorts of classes."

"I thought he was a science guy."

"Poet-geologist. Try this." He handed me a spoonful of the pie filling.

"Oh, my God!"

"Right? Does it need pepper?"

"I don't think so."

"Here. Knead." He pushed the shortbread dough toward me across the stainless-steel tabletop.

I ground my knuckles into the ball.

"How come you don't have a steady?"

"No one ever makes me want to stay in one place."

"Tell me you're not here running away from some man. I cannot have anyone show up; Tom will have to fight him."

"Sounds romantic. Okay, yes, I'm running, just not like that."

"How long has it been?"

"Two years. Since I left home."

"Jesus. You must be dying. Come to think of it, I might know a guy. Big and strong."

"Oh?"

"All right, Little Miss Innocent. What do you think of my brother? I saw you two during the music the other night."

"We were just talking."

"He made eyes at you for three feckin' hours. In my book, that's more than talking." He sprinkled flour on the table, took the dough from my hands, and rolled it into a pie pan.

"No girlfriend?"

"No girlfriend."

"Is he…"

"…A fuckboy?"

"Where's the craic?" Tom said from behind us. He dropped a duffel on the floor with a soggy thump, a bag of Taytos in his hand.

"Hey, captain," Declan smiled. He slid the crust into the oven.

"Hi," I said. I waved and shook flour onto my shirt.

Every time I saw him, he was rain-soaked, sunburnt, and stubbly.

"Pork Pie Time?" Tommy said.

He washed his hands at the sink and winced at the hot water on his raw palms. I wanted to examine them, but refrained.

"Yup," Declan said. "When did you get back?"

"Just now. I'm knackered. It's pissing rain. I haven't seen the sun in ten fecking days. I think I've got scurvy."

"Rickets."

"Right, whatever. Depressing as hell. That smells so good! Tell me there's something left over from earlier."

"I'll get it, don't you touch!" Declan exited into the walk-in cooler. Tom sipped his brother's kombucha.

"How was your trip?" I asked.

"Turbulent. Celtic Sea was choppy. Good fetch, though. How's the clinic?"

"Busy."

Declan returned with a slice of meatloaf, which we watched Tom gulp down cold, then took the crust from the oven and stirred the pie base in.

"How was the sailing?"

"Grand. An east wind brought the sunshine. My favorite."

The men I'd met at school or in another wing of the hospital were the type to take melatonin and hang blackout curtains on their bedroom windows. Tom had probably never even heard of blackout curtains.

"Where did Pork Pie Time come from?"

"It's a secret Archer family tradition," Declan said. "It came from nights when Maude was away and our da was left to cook."

"We were desperate," Tom said.

"Burned Hot Pockets."

"Room temperature soup from the can."

"Frozen pizza with canned mushrooms dumped on."

"Spray cheese."

"We'd have starved if Declan hadn't learned to cook."

"Started as our secret but grew into a habit."

"Nothing like a pork pie after sundown," Tom said.

Declan nodded. "We've an hour 'till we eat. Let's warm up."

We entered the pub and sat.

"You guys are lucky," I said.

"How so?" Declan said.

"You have this pub. Back in the States my shifts would be ten, twelve hours long. I'd get off right as everyone else was having breakfast."

"Did you like working nights?" Tom asked.

I could see him as an old man nodding by the fire. Yeats: "the pilgrim soul in you. The sorrows of your changing face."

"It was all right," I said. "Quieter than the days."

"Cheers to that," Tom said. "My days start at four. It's the twenty of us or so, down at the pier."

"Feckin' loud, they all are," Declan said. "Do they wake you, Frances?"

"I haven't heard them. And I'm a light sleeper."

"We've always been early risers, Tom and me," Declan said.

"It's grand," Tom said. "Slipping out, just darkness and mist to keep you company."

"And yer Sam," Declan said.

"One of my men," Tom said.

"Sam's wild," Declan whispered. "Ladies' man. Unlike my brother here. Might want to watch out, Frannie."

Tom shot Declan a look.

"Do you have a favorite spot to catch fish?"

Tom's mouth turned up at the corners. "Thinking of taking up fishing?"

"Need a backup if the clinic doesn't work out."

"Who was that Galway fisherwoman?" Declan asked.

"Olga," Tom said. "Ninety years old. Still the best nets on the coast."

"She carries a pistol," Declan said.

"Rumor," Tom rolled his eyes. "The old timers said she'd shoot your keel if you took her best fishing spot."

"Not a rumor," Declan said.

"We all have our spots on the coast," Tom said. "People get picky is all. You need an early start. Dawning half-light is best. It's when the fish are first up to feed. It's also the best time to spot a whale if you're wanting to. You can see the humpbacks if you sail south past Dingle. Took Declan out once." He put his hand on Declan's shoulder. "He saw a beautiful Minke near Cork, didn't you? Declan was off the rails the whole day."

"I told you, I'm a creature of land," Declan said. He stood and checked on the pork.

"We sail for a few hours. South usually. Pick up the gulls once we shoot our nets in and start our towing. That's all before six a.m., most days."

"Tommy, can I trouble you for a pint?" one of the older men beside us said. "Your man is back with the dinner, and we're bone dry."

"No trouble at all, Colin," Tom said. He stood and drew pints of Guinness. "Oh, and Colin, this here's Frances."

"How are you, Frances?" Colin asked, reaching an arthritic hand toward mine. "This here is Brendan."

"You've treated my niece at the clinic," Brendan said. "She said you were very nice. But your accent's so thick she could barely understand you."

"I've been working on that."

Declan came back with the pie.

"Jesus, Mary, and Joseph, will you look at that," Colin said. Declan handed me a plate.

"Don't wait. Try it." I blew on the fork. The men watched me chew.

"This is better than Thanksgiving."

"I've heard of it," Colin said. "The hotels put those on."

"Heard of what?" Tom asked.

"Thanksgiving," I said. "It's a holiday in the States."

"And what part of America do you come from?" Brendan asked.

"Heartland. Right in the middle."

"Never been," Brendan said.

"Brendan's never been to the mainland of Ireland," Colin said. "Prefers to stay close to Kathleen."

"Your wife?"

"My Labrador retriever."

Declan untied his apron and sat down by the fire. "There was an American in my first year at Paul Bocuse who cooked a traditional Thanksgiving dinner for the ten of us."

Tom came back with three pints in his hands. He set two before Colin and Brendan, and one in front of him and me.

"Split it?" he asked. I nodded.

"She told us dinner would start at one-thirty."

"Before afternoon tea?" said Colin.

"She was off her rocker. No one showed up until after seven."

Brendan laughed. "What did she cook for you so?"

"Turkey. Must have been the biggest bird in France. Twenty pounds. She had to wake up before dawn to start the tiny oven we had. And there was dinde farce. I forgot the name in English. Just stale bread really."

"Stuffing."

"Right. She used fresh sage. My favorite was the haricots verts à la crème. Help me out, Frances."

"Green bean casserole. Did she add fried onions on top?"

I took off my sweater in the heat from the fire. I felt a familiar sensation. It's winter and I'm at the top of the hill after a big snow. It's after dark, and we're all there. There's been a blizzard. We've taken the truck to St. Martin's at the top of Sulphur Spring Road. Car headlights shine down the hill on all the fresh powder. Midnight. The kids line up for their turn on the snow. My dad and I share a sled, me in front, going so fast our laughter dispels our fear. His big mittens hold my belly too tight. We speed down.

"Yeah! From a can her mother sent her. Probably cost thirty Euros to ship them. But absolutely delicious. And get this. Three types of potatoes."

"Three types," Colin said, and took a long swallow.

"Declan, for the love of Christ, reproduce that meal, why don't you?" Tom asked. "Frances, you can advise him." He took a drink and handed me the pint. When no one was looking I placed my lips on the spot where his lips had been.

"Fair enough," Declan said. "But we aren't eating cranberry slime that comes out of the can in a blob shaped like a can. Abomination. I'm making it fresh."

Tom patted Declan on the back. "I want one whole bird. And all of the potatoes."

"Certainly, all of the potatoes," Brendan said.

18

...

Our last patient before closing time that Saturday was a teen who showed up alone for a Well Woman because her mother, not grasping that her endometriosis kept her from attending school, considered birth control tantamount to the flames of Hell. Having mounted steadily as we inched toward the end of the week, Brigid's spirits peaked while the girl rode off on her bicycle, and she announced that she'd made plans that night "to watch a movie, which is what he calls a date."

Brigid's husband, the tallest man on Inis Mór, styled a silver pompadour over his fine ruddy features with a comb he kept in his shirt pocket, brought Brigid chocolates when he picked her up after work, and devoured her with his eyes while she puttered around the tiny office.

"I don't suppose the island abounds with options for dinner and dancing," I said.

"I suggested Galway," she sighed, "but he hates big cities."

"How'd you two meet?"

"Crib love."

"Adorable."

"Pff. Our mothers were best friends. We were betrothed in the womb. I witnessed his first steps and his first word. Had no choice but to love me till the end of time."

"You never dated anyone else?"

"Never."

"I'm envious."

"It's old-fashioned. The pickings were slim hereabouts, you've no idea. When I left for uni in Cork, he tagged along."

"That's wonderful."

"It's boring."

"A surplus of candidates is worse."

"There may be a surplus, but how many candidates?"

"It's all swiping on apps. You get started with someone. Then he votes the wrong way, likes the wrong kind of music, you trade him in, he trades you, it starts over."

"What about you?"

"Abysmal."

"Met anyone here?"

"No one since the States."

"Come on, Frances. Everyone wants to know which of our men you're planning to marry."

"The one who fetches me at work with chocolate will have my heart."

In Brigid's presence, I doubted I'd ever been in love. If I stayed single, I reassured myself, that would be because trouble followed the men in my life, and I couldn't tell the good ones from the bad.

"Aran men are lovers."

"The guys in the pub where I worked only talked football."

"Aran, not Irish."

"That's the difference?"

"What about Tommy Archer?"

"Nice guy."

"There's talk about how he looks at you."

"Is there?"

"His mother mentioned it."

"What did she say?"

"Chatty Cathy! Want a lift?"

"I'm biking back. Brigid, what did she say?"

"She overheard Tommy tell Declan you were a right feek."

"A feek."

"A stunner."

"I haven't seen him in days."

"He's off catching fish."

"He hasn't done a thing to indicate any interest."

"He might give you a call if you had a phone."

"I'm across the street from him!"

"Frances, Tommy is a gentleman. He's also a cautious boy who's had his heart broken."

"He mentioned that."

"There was a woman not too long ago. She left for London. Comes back at Christmastime. Her family lives on the other side of the island."

"He's dreamy."

"Handsome lad."

I shut down the computer. Brigid turned off the lights. She squeaked open her rusty car door.

"Please don't say anything."

"I love a good romance around here," she winked, settling into the driver's seat. "And don't worry. My lips are sealed."

On my ride home I circled north to Trá Mhór, where I parked by a worker harvesting seaweed on the sand dunes and sat on a piece of driftwood near the shore. Dazzling orange sun obscured the whitecaps. I sketched a young couple walking hand in hand, the cold surf around their knees. I saw Tom in my mind's eye with a faceless woman, and sketched his hands around a cup of tea. What was she like? Why would she leave him? I drew Toby's hands holding his basketball. I outlined Seán. At dusk I took the road south to Maude's.

A right feek.

I parked and walked to the pub, blowing on my hands to warm them. Men shouted at the soccer game, groaned in unison, and dispersed.

Tom sat across from me.

"Did you see that play?" he asked.

"I saw the effect it had on Tom Senior. He looks like he could use a good cry."

"I've been out to sea. Have you missed me?"

"Immensely."

"What's the craic?"

"We had a goring incident."

"Goat?"

"Name of Seamus."

"Lot of boys named that."

"It's the goat's name. How were the waters?"

"Deadly. In Galway I saw an old football mate from uni. He's an engineer now."

"He quit football?"

"He met a British girl. They're having their second baby soon enough. Said he likes his knees without injury. He has city hands now."

"You're no fan of city hands, or babies."

"I've no experience with either."

"If you met a nice girl you might have some babies."

"Tried that. Didn't work out."

"The babies or the girl?"

"City blokes bring more to the table."

"Her loss."

"She gave the ring back, at least."

"Well, that's good."

"Maude didn't care much for her anyway."

"Mother knows best."

"What about you?"

My high school boyfriend now worked as an attorney representing marijuana farmers in Oregon. Every experience I had after him amounted to the sort of smoldering allure that passed for synchronicity, but scorched on contact. Too mysterious to touch, too physical to avoid.

"A few entanglements. No engagements."

My whole adult life, the threat of anger had warded me off. They looked the way they looked, they said the things they said, and every one of them, even the ones like my dad, had an Anton in him. Angie, my college roommate, followed my boyfriend on social media. One Saturday morning, waving a spatula in the air and scrolling through his Instagram, she asked, "Where's Frances in this lineup?" and turned her phone around to show me a photo of him with his arm around a girl in a Budweiser tube dress at the party he'd gone to two weekends before in the next college town while I was on an overnight at this hospital. For all that, not so surprisingly, men were inconsequential.

"Have you always lived here?"

"Left for uni for a bit. Then, before I got my own boat, me and my mate Sam spent some time on the mainland working winters on the quay."

"Sounds like hard work."

"Savage. The first month was long shifts boxing herring. Fifty tons a night, some nights."

"Dublin?"

"Donegal. It's one of the highest-grossing fishing ports in Ireland. I had to perfect my trade. Sometimes the bosses didn't care if we clowned about, as long as the fish were ready for market the following morning. Sam would swear at them, but they'd just come back with a quip and a wicked grin and another line of boxes stacked four or five high."

I nodded, imagining him lifting crates of herring on a windy dock. A line of sweat on the back of his shirt. His spine, bent over his boots. His laughter from across the bar. His shoulders, tired after a day.

"They were fourteen-hour night shifts. I spent the season lifting forty-kilo boxes of fish. That howling east wind was cold, and I thought I could do it forever. It paid time-and-a-half and you were too tired to spend your wages. Exhaustion blotted out your mind. Some shifts we moved a million pounds by dawn. After a few months, I went out on larger trawlers, beamers. They go for five, ten days, all around the local waters, and land their catch. That was right before I came back to work with me da."

"Was it lonely out there for so long?"

"Not at all. I filled my locker with secondhand books."

"Plus a pinup girl?"

"Hula dancer! Always wiggling, that one. The sea may be cold, but it's never still."

"Did you name her?"

"Never named her. You know, there were moments when I could step out the door and predict exactly how the wind would affect the shore. Tides too."

"Like an extra sense. Of course you know about wind. It's your business to know."

"My bedroom window faced east-northeast. That's my favorite."

"You have a favorite wind?"

"Aye, east-northeast."

He drew a pipe from his jacket and turned it in his hands.

"I wonder what direction my window faces."

"South-southeast. Toward Galway Bay."

"Fishing in the dark sounds intense."

"Yeah. It caught up with me after a while. Look at me talking all about myself like a sop."

"My window in the States was east-facing. Full of sunlight just as I was getting home from work."

"What was it like?"

"Thinking on your feet. Your patient's blood pressure plunges. Vitals all over the place. Or it's a false alarm and their arterial line just needs replacing or adjusting. They need their throats suctioned. They need more pressors. They need CPR. They live, they die. Or worse, they live with the extent of their injuries. Damaged lungs, broken alveoli, leaking cerebrospinal fluid, blown pupils. Fates worse than death."

"Did you have a lot of patients who didn't make it?"

"Yes, I did."

"Did you have to zip them up?

"Yeah."

"Was that the hardest part?"

"They're at peace when they pass. But life is where the suffering is. Broken bodies. Parents asking why God took their child."

"I see why you'd want to get away from all that."

"I was the last to witness someone at least once a week. It's always so quiet in the room after a patient dies. Just a body with a toe tag. No more beeps from IV poles. Speaking of danger, have you ever been out in a storm?"

"Plenty of times."

"When I was researching Inis Mór, I saw videos of boats tossed on the waves."

"Once, about a year back, there was a warm spell off the west coast of Britain, massive high seas and wind. It was like we were being chased, waves like mountains. One afternoon the they were so high, and the bow was moving so far up and down, two of my mates got sick, and with one dip, we went down into the wave, and struggled to pull up from under the sea, and the water surged from both sides, over and over, running everywhere over the deck. We made it through, but the trip took a toll. As we came alongside the quay, the dockies stared with their mouths open; the ship had taken such a battering."

"Didn't that scare you?"

"In a strange way, it was beautiful."

"I'll stick to land."

"You'll get to know the water here. That way, it won't frighten you. Start with a swim maybe. Do you plan to stay for a while?"

"For now, at least."

"Don't you miss home?"

"I'm just doing my own thing. My mom may visit one day."

"Do you get on with her?"

"I do."

"What about your da?"

"He died a long time ago."

"Sorry to hear it."

"Brigid treated an American today who'd been injured while diving."

"Yeah, they come here for that. They love the Wormhole."

"Sounds daunting."

"Poll na bPéist. It's a pool just south of Dún Aonghasa. Totally natural, but looks man-made. It fills up with the tide. People come from all over to dive into it."

"Just like the YMCA."

"You're not here for the Wormhole."

"No, I'm not. No good with the elements."

"In that case, I prescribe a visit to Kilmurvey."

"What's that?"

"It's a beach down the way. Like the French Riviera, but colder. Honestly, though, it's brilliant. I can give you a few tips if you'd like. Treading water, simple strokes, you know."

"I know how to swim."

"Ever swam in the ocean?"

I shook my head.

"You need to learn to tread water at least. It's important if you're staying on. You working tomorrow?"

"The clinic is closed on the Lord's day. All ailments must wait until Monday morning."

"Perfect. I'll pick you up before breakfast. Let's say eight o'clock."

"I don't have a swimsuit."

"T-shirt, you know, whatever works. Oh, and one more thing. Would it be all right if I called you Frannie?"

"Not Frances?"

"You're grand. Beautiful name. Just feels formal. Anyone else call you Frannie?"

"No."

"So it can be just mine. I'm the only one who gets to call you that."

"The only one?"

"That's right. What do you say?"

"Sure, you can call me Frannie."

19

...

Dawn lit the film of dust that coated the box lid. "I have a date," I told my dad. "Fisherman. Has a good handshake. Wish me luck." I rummaged the drawer, chose a pair of shorts, put the sweater and a scarf over my tank top, and wheeled my bike to the pub. Tom pedaled up to the curb with half a piece of toast in his mouth and Michael Collins trotting along behind.

"Feeling hardy?"

"Yep."

He opened the door, and Michael Collins scurried inside, where Maude was pouring tea for two men in burglar caps. "No dogs on the beach, big fella."

He blew on his hands and rubbed them together. "Ready?"

"I'm all yours."

"Grand. Let's head off."

For twenty minutes we rode west on the coastal road through a stiff wind to a beach alongside a pond sheltered by cottages. Gulls loitered on driftwood or floated on the water, still asleep, heads under their wings. We parked at a stone wall where a boy sat fiddling out of tune.

Tom reached into his bag and handed me a thermos.

"Black with sugar, right?"

"You remembered."

"Did I make it right?"

"Too sweet."

"You don't like it."

"I do. It was thoughtful of you to make it for me."

"No trouble at all."

We made our way toward the water.

"I'll never understand coffee drinkers."

"What's to understand?"

"The taste. Just not my thing."

"Maybe you haven't had the right cup."

"Coffee is all the same."

"Not true."

"Just bean water if you think about it. Try mine?"

I placed my mouth where his had been.

"That's Irish Breakfast," he said.

"Not bad. Is it Barry's?"

"You like Barry's?"

"Out of all the teas Declan has made me try, it's the winner."

"You've got good taste."

Church bells rang across the street. Elderly couples exited mass arm in arm, their hands reaching for the priest's.

Tom laid his towel out. I followed suit.

"Do you bring that everywhere you go?" he asked, nodding at my sketchbook.

"I like drawing the places I see."

"More than taking photos?"

"It lets me remember things better."

"Music is like that too. See that land over there?"

"Yeah," I said.

"Those ridges are the Dunes. They're glacial sediments. Tens of thousands of years old, they are. Always changing. Not one of them is the same today as it was yesterday."

"Because of the wind?"

"Yeah. Saltmarsh to the north there," he pointed. "Full of heath-dog, saltwort, plants that love the salty air. I thought of them because of your sketchbook. They have a great importance to those of us in the West. Mayo particularly. During the Great Hunger, people couldn't bury their dead. Either didn't have the land or the strength. So they buried them in the dunes. Shane McGowan wrote a song about it. Want to listen?"

"I do."

Tom typed on a cracked iPhone and handed it to me. An image of dunes filled the screen. The singer's fierce baritone rose from the tinny speaker and sang a ballad in a minor key a cappella. In three verses the song said burial in the dunes held out a promise of heaven that the wind and rain revealed to be false.

"Who's the singer?" I asked.

"Ronnie Drew. I got off point there. What I meant to say is, I think it's grand that you sketch, you know?"

"Why is that?"

"Because it preserves the image. You know, for the next generation. I feel that way about poems. Well, come on." He took off his sweater and reached out to me. "Nothing to be afraid of."

"What if the current drags me away?"

"Won't let it happen. I promise."

We took off our outer clothing.

"Stay close, you hear? This isn't a swimming pool. Keep your wits about you." I followed and glimpsed the hair down the center of his torso.

The last time I went swimming, during my final year of nursing school, I'd done laps in a pool to get away from the cries, the beeping, the chatter, and the squeak of shoes work. This sea, its foam, the tide, and cold waves, things under the moon's command, by contrast, could swallow me up.

"Ready? It's okay if you're afraid. But you have to know how to go about in this water. It's important. Trust me."

I nodded. He held out his hand and walked me to the sea.

We waded in up to our knees, thighs, waists. When he dove I did too. We surfaced at the same time.

"You all right?" he asked. Brown freckles collected in a birthmark on his chest. I reached out and touched it. I wanted to press my lips to it.

We waded out. Others had arrived at the beach. Children ran into the water, parents in tow, voices ringing out.

"You're grand," he said. "A natural."

"Thanks."

"So how long do you plan to stay in that little room of Wanda's?"

"Brigid wants me to stay on. Why?"

He reached for me as the next swell rose between us. I held onto him. "I get the feeling you're running from something. People come here for that. Brokenhearted women. Men looking to be heroes by diving in the Wormhole."

I squinted up at him. "Yes, I'm here for the Wormhole!"

"Are you running? Because you know, in the end, wherever you go, there you are."

"I think we're all running from something."

"Probably. Why'd you choose here?"

"Because of a book of poems."

"By who?"

"Yeats."

"'The Lake Isle of Innisfree'?"

"The bees in the glade."

"That poem is about County Sligo."

"That's where my dad grew up."

"Is that why you came?"

"That's one reason. I brought his ashes with me."

"Do you plan to lay him to rest in Sligo then?"

"Yes, but not yet."

"If you need a lift to the mainland, I might know someone with a boat."

"I'll keep that in mind."

"Now, way out here, what do you do if you get tired?"

"Swim to shore?"

"Too tired to tread water, too tired to swim."

"I don't know."

He lay on his back, arms relaxed. "Float like this." Breath rose and sank in his chest. He stood. "You try."

I tried to float like him, but my head went under the next wave, and I coughed.

"Here," he said, putting his arm around me. "Try again." I leaned back, looked up, and lowered my head beneath the surface upside down. Silence cut off the children and the fiddle. Tom held one hand under the nape of my neck and the other under the small of my back. Eclipsing the sun, his head was a black silhouette on the sky.

When had I last been touched? The OR nurse in town on a travel contract the month before I left the United States had an Ansel Adams print by the door and a mattress with no give. The touch of his fingers described an anatomy textbook illustration on my skin, and for breakfast the next morning he fed me a slice of cherry pie, which we ate with plastic forks, leaning against his kitchen counter.

Sun glittered on Tom's shoulders. His eyes stared into the distance. I felt lust like hunger. Or the hunger felt me, became me. In my head I saw our two seaborne shapes far below, a duo of nuclei, motes divided from a speck split into further pairs in an act of mitotic love, of which we were the first dividers, originals of a passion that would outstrip ourselves and belong to ocean, earth, sky. Trillions enclosed in a plasma membrane, communicating with cells around it, not unlike the glance, touch, emotion, not unlike how deoxyribonucleic acid copies itself, exponential growth, cellular signals, mutations, communities.

What had begun as a queasy glance on the ferry washed over me now. I listened from underwater. We stayed like that until another swell lifted and pushed us together. Our eyes met, his hand against my spine, my chest against his. Our lips parted. I squinted at his eyes, his lashes. I pressed a finger to the scar on the pink skin of his upper lip. He tensed up, released me, pushed a strand of hair from my forehead. His palm settled against my temple, then caressed my cheek. We moved apart and waded toward shore. I labored dizzily through the surf, and he followed. We stepped onto the warm sand, his hand on mine, the wind sharp.

If I were a priestess, I told myself, I would consecrate the temple of my faith to this beach, this day.

I sat on the towel, and he spread the other towel over my shoulders and plopped down next to me, and we stayed that way, and I didn't think of anything but the sand holding us up from underneath.

20

...

"How often do you get to Inis Oírr?"

Brigid had spent the morning stitching up an English woman who'd fallen on the cobblestone sidewalk outside Joe Mac's, then tried to stanch the gash on her chin with a guayabera, and now lay on a cot with an ice pack on her forehead, having just returned to the village after taking "the perfect engagement photo at the cliffs." Her fiancé stood out front, cigarette dangling, cell phone in hand, a small topless monument to something or other.

"About once a month. Set to go Monday. Fiona Dermot is due her prednisone."

"Can I go along? I've been reading about Saint Ghobnait and I want to see her beehive."

"You can go in my stead if you'd like. I usually ride over on one of the fishermen's boats. But one of us has to staff the clinic for the day."

"I'll go, if you don't mind."

"Not at all. But be warned. Fiona lives with her very nearly deaf husband. You'll be forced to have dinner with them. You won't be back before dark."

"Is that so bad?"

"You'll see."

A jumble of blurry snapshots—stone house, man's pudgy face, woman hanging laundry—sum up my trip back. Along the way I stopped at the McAulay gate. "I brought you an apple," I said to the gray fetlock, flank, snout, eye. A donkey was my dad's favorite animal on the farm growing up.

My father's hands and feet were giant. He lined up his chukkas in a closet, where I wandered among belts and a shoe shine box. I slid my feet into his shoes and shuffled down the hallway as Tick-Tack barked at my heels. Reading the paper next to the green library lamp, glasses on the end of his nose, Dad would look up at me and smile as I walked to and fro in front of him, not guessing that one day he would die.

After the funeral, people ate the food spread out on the table and leafed through the photo album. Mom was pale and quiet in her black dress. Voices floated upstairs to where I sat, scraping my knuckles against the brick wall. I crept to my father's closet, closed the door, and sat beside a stack of carpentry magazines. With my finger on a boot I traced the outline of his toe. I thought about how a body could be there, and not there.

We stopped eating dinner in the kitchen and took our plates to the living room, where we watched television on the couch with Tick-Tack. Mom let me sleep with her in her bed, and we kept the windows open.

Then Mom met Anton. She and I said even less to each other after that.

My livestock hadn't backed up traffic, I hadn't delivered a homily, and I hadn't committed a tourist's follies, so no one on Inis Mór asked me any hard questions. No one cared what I'd done or not done. I was invisible. I'd disappeared.

It had been six weeks since I first met Tom, five weeks and four days since I started work in Brigid's clinic, two weeks since Tom first reached for my hand. In the past week, I'd opened an account at the credit union on Lower Kilronan, ordered coffee and a Chemex from the mainland, and received my replacement passport. I still had no phone. I could be reached in person at Wanda's or at the clinic, or by phone on Wanda's landline or Brigid's cell.

Privacy meant I could stay here with my bike and my cliffs, instead of my car and my city, and maybe someday with my stone house, my window overlooking the sea, and my donkey, who I would name after the summer rain that has no past.

21

...

On Kilronan pier, men sat mending a net alongside brightly painted boats. Tom Junior stood nearby, coat tied around his waist, thermal clinging to his stomach. He waved.

"Morning."

"How are ya, Frances?"

"Hiya, Frannie."

"This your Dad's?"

"Aye. His wee *Carmona*."

"Inis Oírr is grand this time of year." Tom Senior lifted a crate to a crewman, took my bag from Tom Junior, and stepped onto his vessel.

"What does that say?" I pointed to a phrase on the port side.

"'Archer's Boat.' Clever, yeah?" Tom climbed up beside his father.

"You can write Irish?"

"It's my second most practical skill. Step beyond the side there." He hoisted me on board. The space contained rod holders, coiled rope, and bait tanks. A small cabin faced the foredeck.

"Irish is the oldest language in the whole west of Europe," Tom Senior said. "Only half of us know how to speak it, though."

"My dad knew it."

"Did you learn at all?"

"Wish I did."

"Have Tommy teach you."

Tom Senior pocketed his compass. I gripped the gunwale.

"We'll get right on that, da."

"Did you learn in school or from your parents?"

"Both. Maude made certain. Old timers are committed!"

"Who're you calling 'old timer'? A hundred years ago, speaking Irish was punishable, due to the Troubles and all. But the islanders never lost it. Tommy's first word was in Irish."

"What was it?"

"Athair. 'Father.' I was so proud. Though if you ask Maude, it came out sounding more like a sneeze."

"Sore spot for ma. Best not speak of it."

"Frances, you can sit inside there. More comfortable than the last boat we were on together."

"I feel fine today."

"Tommy, take her up to the cuddy."

"Aye, captain."

I followed Tom Junior. Inside the cabin he stored a fire extinguisher in stowage, moved a pair of boots from a bench, and dropped my bag.

"Glad to have you along today," he said. "Back in a minute. Systems check."

He patted me on the shoulder and climbed back down.

"Welcome aboard," Tom Senior said. "Bathroom is that way if you need it." He sat in front of some gadgets and screens, turned a key, and the engine engaged. I leaned against the faded wheelhouse wall and watched Tom Junior stack mats on the deck below. Tom Senior peered over his dashboard. "Can't wait for some of Fiona's pudding."

"What's that?"

"Drisheen. Delicious, it is. Have you had it?"

"Afraid not."

"We'll sail for a little over an hour. Make yourself at home."

We backed out of the slip and glided into the misty channel. I chose a seat facing aft and sipped my coffee. The crab pots bounced, and Tom Junior secured them. The wake stretched out. Cill Rónáin pier shrank.

Tom Junior rejoined us, stomping his boots and closing the cabin door. "How's it looking?" He squinted over Tom Senior's shoulder at a screen where red and blue lines streaked a black field.

"Traffic," Tom Senior said. "Some fishermen, some cargo en route to Cork." He zoomed out to show a map with dozens of small triangles, each indicating the position of a ship relative to the Irish mainland and the island of Great Britain.

"How often do you make this trip?"

"Once every couple months," Tom Junior said. "Inis Oírr's population is below three hundred. We mostly deliver supplies."

"We're in Galway more often," Tom Senior said. "Which is how we made your acquaintance."

"That feels like ages ago."

"Tommy will give you the grand tour while I'm conducting my business."

"Business, my arse."

"Watch your tongue, we've a lady with us. Anyway, my plan is to drop my nets and have a pint with Willy D., assuming the slow boaters don't hinder our journey."

"Sail boaters, that is." Tom Junior lowered two teabags into his thermos and sat. His father steered us past cliffs where birds nested in ventifacts.

The port comprised two slips and the sky. Mr. William Dermot, Willy D., stood at the end of the pier, a spotted hound at his feet. He held a crumpled bag of sunflower seeds whose shells he spat over the side at a flock of gulls. The dog eyed our approach.

"Is that dog named Robert Emmet?"

"Not at all," Tom Junior said, coiling a rope around his arm. "That's Enya."

"Dia duit!" William shouted. "Howya, Tom?"

"Howya, William?"

"Look, Frances—Caisleán O'Brien!"

A ruined castle sat atop a distant hill, beyond whose slopes lay a vast emptiness. Stones punctuated the turf, and sun glinted on the water. We followed William and Enya inland past a ship's rusted hull that had run aground on the ruderal shore.

Fiona Dermot's house presided over a churchyard of skewed headstones. We ducked inside. A small pot hung simmering over a peat fire next to bacon frying in a cast-iron pan. Fiona sliced tomatoes. Under a plaid shawl, slung around the neck of a woman about my age, an infant squirmed. The men removed their caps. Fiona wiped her hands on her apron. She kissed her husband, then Enya, Tom Senior, Tom Junior, and me.

"How are ya, Tommy?"

"Grand. How are things?"

"Lovely. Hiya, Frances, I'm Fiona. This here's Nora and baby Rowan."

"How are youse?" Nora waved, and Rowan pumped his legs.

"Brigid said you'd be coming. Thanks so much for bringing my medicine along so."

"My pleasure. I'd like to go over it, if you have a minute."

"Not to worry, dear, I Googled the side effects."

"Do you have any questions?"

Older patients on the island often tried to avoid being told how and when to take their medication. I listed the symptoms that would warrant a call to Brigid, and Fiona turned toward her stove, reached into a salt cellar, sprinkled the sliced tomatoes, and licked her fingers.

"What's the news, Tom? Aren't you starved?"

Nora's cell phone rang. The baby squirmed.

"Ma, take him, will ya?" Nora said. Fiona lifted the child and limped to the hearth where I stood.

"Hold this wee one for a minute, please, Frances, while I finish up here." I dandled him, and he gazed up and chewed his fist. His mother talked on the phone around the corner. I shrugged in mock helplessness at Tom Junior, and he laughed and poured himself a glass of beer from a mason jar.

"Let's see that sausage," Tom Senior said, and peeked into Fiona's pot.

I bounced the baby, who gurgled and watched his mother.

Around the way, a young couple had recently inherited an uncle's farm, Fiona told us, and the property was surely haunted, she said, because you could hear "wailing at all hours of the night."

"Agh, that's a sign," Tom Senior said.

I perused the books, all in Gaelic, on a bookshelf in the corner. Tom Junior walked up behind me, and I felt his palm warm on my arm.

"How are ya, little man?"

Rowan assessed the situation and considered whether he should cry.

"You like kids?"

"Sure. This guy reminds me of my brother."

Rowan kicked and smiled. Tom Junior touched his foot.

"You've got to be careful around here. People will just hand you their offspring."

Nora appeared beside us and reached for Rowan. "Thanks," she said. "That was his da."

"He coming?"

She rolled her eyes. "His truck's stuck in Fhormna."

"Shite. Did he get a tow?"

"He's waiting out the tide at the pub." She walked off. The fire popped. Tom Junior turned to me.

"Care for a sip?"

I shook my head.

"How about a look around the island? Unless you're hungry, that is." He nodded towards Fiona's hearth.

"What's in the pot?"

"Black pudding."

"A tour sounds great."

"Take her to St. Kevin's," Fiona said over William's shoulder. "We'll hold some sausage for your ride home."

"That's grand. She's been reading about Cill Ghobnait, so I'd like to show her that as well."

I looked up. Tom winked.

Fiona turned to me again and lowered her voice. "Ghobnait fled here after a row with her family. They say visiting her church brings you peace." Then, to Tom Junior, "It's just so good to see

you out and about again. We've missed you." She held his face in
both hands.

"Thanks, Fiona." He smiled, looking down, and drained his
glass. "Ready then?"

"Is it impolite for me to turn down the pudding?" We passed
Enya stretched out by the fire.

"Famine fare." He buttoned his sweater and held the door,
and I took a deep breath of salt air. "The stock is made from pigs'
blood. I practically grew up on it. Have you tried?"

I shook my head.

"Come on. I'll take you around, and then we can grab
something at the pub."

We walked into a world of grey. Tom led us off the empty
main road toward a sunken ruin, overgrown with grass and
surrounded by mossy Celtic crosses. The sign read 'ST.
CHAOMHÁIN'S.' A woman stood nibbling a scone wrapped in
parchment. A child in a sweater toddled at her feet.

"It's pronounced 'Kevin's.' Thousand years old at least. Lots
of ghost stories, if you're into that kind of thing."

He took a pipe from his pocket, dropped tobacco into it from
a pouch, and stuck it in his mouth. Then he took off his scarf and
hung it around my neck. He lifted my hair and tied a loose knot
at my throat. Heat rose in my limbs. I felt his warmth on the
wool. He'd stepped close enough for me to smell the unlit
tobacco in the pipe and see the lines around his eyes, the scar
across his lip. He took a strand of my hair between his thumb
and forefinger.

"Hippocastanum. Irish Chestnut. Its seed is the color of your
hair. Might be even darker. Nearly raven-haired. Beautiful, but
deadly."

I looked into his face. We'd touch if he leaned forward.

"That means excellent."

"Thanks."

"No trouble at all. Got to keep a scarf on you at all times.
Don't want to catch a cold now, do you?" He looked at my lips,
then my eyes.

We wandered the site in silence.

"Ruins, ghosts, this island has everything. Declan must love it here."

"You and Declan get on well." He drew a box of matches from his pocket.

"Did you know most oral cancers are caused by tobacco use?"

"Every captain has to have a pipe every now and again." He struck a match against a stone, brought the flame to the bowl, and took a puff. "Let's see the view from the vestibule."

Through an arch the afternoon sun illuminated a pile of leaves in an alcove. Tom pointed to a plot of tall greens encircling the church. "See this here? Grass of Parnassus. It grows all over. Loves the limestone. Ten years ago the government worked with the farmers to clear out the boreens. They got rid of the scrub, and cleaned up the landscape."

I fingered a small white flower with a yellow center. "This looks like hawthorn."

"It is."

"That's the Missouri state flower."

"No kidding. The Irish are superstitious about hawthorn." He crouched to enter the main part of the priest's nave.

"How come?"

"Old myths. They were called faerie trees. You couldn't cut them down without angering the faeries."

"You're a tour guide today."

"I've been meaning to ask. Why only one cow? They're social animals. They like a herd." He crossed one leg over the other, tapped his pipe on the stone, refilled and relit it.

"I could manage two. Maybe sisters."

"Two is better." He blew smoke from the side of his mouth.

I sat next to him, and he put an arm around my shoulders.

"Hungry yet?"

"For famine fare, or pub fare?"

"Pub," he said. "Those foods are all right. It wasn't a famine. Famine is when nothing grows. Plenty of things grew here. The

96

British just extracted it. They left one thing, though. Potatoes. But those were blighted."

I followed him around the foundation. Examined the vibrant moss between stones as he looked under an arch at the other end.

"People got married here."

"And buried."

"And baptized."

"First Communion."

"First Reconciliation."

"Catholic?"

"Lapsed."

"Have you had full sacraments?"

"I dropped out before Confirmation."

"You don't have a Confirmation name?"

I shook my head.

"Mine's Andrew. Patron saint of fishermen. No confirmation, Jesus, how will my mother ever get beyond that?"

"Let's call for a priest as soon as we get back to Fiona's."

"There's probably one at the pub we're headed to. Ready?"

We returned to the main road and walked in silence until two cyclists asked in English accents how to find the dolphins.

Tom pointed toward a rusted ship's hull beached in a pile of slate on the water. Wind billowed his jacket. "A way down the road, past the wreck there."

"That the *Plassey*?" one of the men asked.

"Aye."

"How did it run aground?"

"Bad storm. Way back so. It was full of whiskey and yarn. Couldn't save the ship, but they managed to salvage the cargo." He winked at me.

"Brilliant!"

We followed. Gulls idled on the bow as we passed. Tom took my hand and we continued wordlessly to Cill Ghobnait.

"Here you go then."

The remains of another church in tall grass. We stood before the ruin, its stones bright in the sun. "There used to be Irish dancing here at the crossroads. My parents brought us."

"You dance?"

"Not at all. Declan, though, he's a natural. Maude used to tell me Ghobnait's bees would chase brigands who tried to get in." He pointed to an ancient beehive.

"I could use bees now and then."

"Couldn't we all. Her clochán is said to be close by."

"How did you know I was reading about Ghobnait?"

"Lucky guess."

"No, really."

"At the pub last weekend you left your book open when you were in the jacks."

"So you like to peek in a lady's book. Just for that, you have to show me one of your poems."

"I've only ever shown them to my mother."

"Just one."

Tom nodded and bit his lip. I turned toward him, looked up, and watched him watch me. I reached for his hand and we walked north to the Tigh Ned, a hundred or so yards from the pier where the *Carmona* was docked.

The pub was a house with picnic benches and bare stone walls. A girl threw a Frisbee to a dog next to a row of bicycles. Inside, two children dressed in bright dancing costumes ignored their mothers, who shifted teething babies from hip to hip. A couple threw darts. Three old men at a table covered with empty pint glasses held fiddles in their laps. Tom led me to the bar.

"Tommy." The bartender's white mustache dangled past his chin.

"How are ya, Podge. This here's Frannie."

"Podge Vinegar. What'll you have?"

"Barry's. Black with sugar."

"Two pints. And a plate of your claws."

The bartender turned to draw the stout.

"Two for you?"

"You'll want a sip."

I followed Tom to a corner table. He clinked his glass against mine.

"What are we toasting?"

"Our first date, of course."

Podge brought my tea and a large crab wrapped in paper. We ate. Tom watched the soccer game.

"How did you get that scar?"

"Which one?"

"On your upper lip."

"That's Declan's. It was the only proper punch the man's ever thrown in his life. He was ten, but it landed. Maude had a fit. Brigid stitched me up."

"Lips are harder to heal. Fewer cellular layers." I ran my finger along the scar.

"Suppose I'm marked forever."

"What did you do to make him punch you?"

"It was practice. I was teaching him how to defend himself. On account of his being bullied. Declan will never admit it, but things haven't always been easy for him. He's the only openly gay man on a conservative island. He needed to know how to keep the thick donkeys away."

"You're a good teacher."

"Too good."

"We see ourselves as different from others, but we're pretty much the same. When you've spent time in the ICU, you don't see much of a difference anymore."

"Tell that to those bleedin' eejits."

"They probably had something to hide."

He fingered his unlit pipe. "I don't buy it. We protect our own."

"The DNA in bone has a half-life of seventeen hundred years. Around half the genetic material from a disaster that took place two or three thousand years ago would still remain today, which is enough to analyze. You know Pompeii, the city that was destroyed when Mount Vesuvius erupted. Did you ever see that image of the two victims, the child in the mother's embrace, the gold bracelet on her arm, both of them encased in burning ash? Well, they studied the victims, and the adult turned out to be a male, and the child wasn't related to him."

"So he comforted a stranger."

"Strangers can treat each other well."

"I'm going to have to teach you to throw a punch, too. You shouldn't be too trusting."

"That would be useful. I was recently robbed, after all."

"Ah, your pickpocket. That's why I like to stay close to my people."

"Do you think you'll ever leave for a city?"

"Prefer the island life. Our ma likes us close. What about you? Thought any more about how long you'll stay?"

"As long as y'all need a nurse."

"'Y'all.' A Yank. You can't board with Wanda forever."

"Maybe I'll try to convince Birdie to sell me her house. Word on the street is she wants to move back to Mayo."

"You keep treating her aching bones, and she might just give it to you. I'm dying to move out of Fishermen's Row. The other day I saw a remote little place that reminded me of T.E. Lawrence's Clouds Hill. Just a wee cottage. I'd be in heaven somewhere like that."

"A wee cottage is a big dream."

"You wouldn't miss the city life?"

"I lived it for twenty-eight years. What I want now is quiet. A fireplace like your mother's. A finger of smoke."

"Finger of smoke. I'm stealing that."

"I want credit."

"What you want is a Goshen."

"Goshen?"

"Sanctuary."

"That's what I want."

"My next place needs to be standalone. I'm tired of hearing my mates shagging. My neighbor Sam is a playboy. Different girl every weekend. It's why I sleep on my boat most nights."

"Not too many women on the island."

"He likes tourists. Picks them out when they're cycling around. I don't mean to paint him in a bad way. He's a decent sort of guy. Saved my life a hundred times."

"What did he do? Steer you away from a storm?"

"That's one way to put it," he said. "Well, I'm glad you've chosen to stay put. Most visitors are gone after a day or two."

"Am I a visitor?"

"Can't tell yet. You're cúthail. You keep your cards close."

"Takes one to know one."

"Perhaps I'm just being cautious."

"About what?"

Old men walked into the pub wearing jerseys over their sweaters and asked the waitress to turn on the Cork City game.

"About getting attached."

The men hollered at the television. Tom leaned in. "Want to take this party to the pier? End of day on the water is my favorite."

I nodded. Tom paid and carried the bag of chips and two cans of Guinness out the door. Halfway through the field adjacent to the pub, I stumbled, and he took my hand. We passed a row of houses where two old men leaned on a low stone wall. A dog ran yapping alongside us. The men nodded at Tommy and me as we passed.

"Something like that so?" He nodded toward the houses.

"That's right."

Back at the pier, Tom reached down from the *Carmona* to lift me aboard.

22

...

He leaned on the rail. I stood against the gunwale.

"Have you always worked on the water?"

"Anything to sail. Nothing against land, I just love the water. Even in howling weather. Some of the fishermen I know worked the cruise ships after a while. Looking to clean up. Smart white uniform and a suntan. But I like being my own boss, getting my hands dirty. What about you? Were you your own boss at the hospital?"

"I had a charge nurse, but I acted independently and took care of my own patients. Working nights left me even more on my own."

"Solitary girl."

"I like the quiet."

"Sometimes when it got too quiet at night on the *Mackerel Yawl*, my mate Scotty would play his guitar on the quarterdeck. He said it brought in the fish. That run, we almost caught a tuna off the Isle of Man, a bluefin snapped my line, and almost broke the rod. So I'd say it worked."

I closed the gap between us in two steps, rested my forearms on his shoulders, and laced my fingers behind his neck.

"Sorry to interrupt."

I brought his mouth to mine.

Stubble on his chin. Tobacco on his tongue. His chapped lips. One hand on the small of my back, the other behind my head, fingers in my hair. I pushed myself up against him. The tighter he held me, the more my grip on myself slackened. The boat rocked in its slip. A bolt of lust struck my body with a force that shook me out of myself and woke the need I'd had for him all this time, elemental as thirst. I reached out for balance, and he held me in place. Then his mouth was back on mine. I tasted his breath. This kiss slowed and deepened, and the heat rose lower.

He felt me all over and moved his lips to my jaw, my neck. He said my name, and I heard myself moan. I groped his chest and felt his heart beating fast through layers of wool.

The heart circulates oxygen, nutrients, hormones, and waste around the body. In adults the heart beats at a rate of sixty to one hundred beats per minute. When we're nervous or excited, signals from our autonomic nervous system, and hormones like epinephrine, cause the heart to speed up. I once overheard a surgeon describe cardiac cellular communication while I was checking the IV during prep for open-heart surgery. The doctor sat beside the patient, and rather than tell him not to worry, said, "A heart cell will pulse on its own if you isolate it in a culture, and if you move two of them close together, they'll synchronize their pulse." The patient asked why, and the doctor said no one knew, but for him, it was the hand of God. I drew a different conclusion from the doctor's operating room biology lesson. To me, such synchrony meant one heart could become another's counterpart, the dearest, most precious heart of all.

Tom lifted me onto a ledge in the cabin, and we wrapped our arms around each other. My legs parted for him, and I drew his hips toward me. I felt his calloused hands on my face, under my sweater, against my back. He panted and his eyes moved over my body, as if to take in as much of me as he could. I reached under the sweater, under the shirt, for his back, and brought his mouth again to mine.

"I almost kissed you when we went for the swim. You're bleedin' massive."

I moved my tongue to his neck, just below the jaw, and tasted salt.

He started to say something, then stopped.

"What is it?"

"Wanted to ask you. Since you'll be staying on for a while. Our swim. What did you think of it?"

"Cold."

"Do you know why I wanted you to learn to float?"

I shook my head.

"Has anyone talked to you about my brother?"

"Maude showed me a photo in the pub."

"So you know he drowned?"

"She told me. He looks like you."

"Maybe so. Better face though. Lad always looked like he was happy with everyone he saw. I need to tell you, when I care about someone, I want them to be safe."

He opened the second can of Guinness and offered it to me. I shook my head.

"I wish I could have met him."

"He was funny, to start. Even as a baby. Even being born. Right after, they brought him out in a pink blanket. I was so excited. Thought I had a sister. But nope, another boy. Brigid was out of blue blankets!"

"I have a little brother. Toby."

"He's lucky to have a nurse for a sister, taking care of everyone."

"Do you remember the day Maude took that photo of him?"

"I do. It was the day of the big rabbit reveal."

"Is that an Aran holiday?"

"More like an Aran pestilence. Seán loved animals. All of them. Wouldn't hurt a fly. If we watched an old movie with a dog in it, he'd get upset and say the dog had died long before then. Years ago the rabbit population on Inis Mór got out of control. There were millions of 'em. They were everywhere, and they took over everything. They ate the grass, and the livestock's food supply dwindled. The old-timers killed some, but those were too full of birdshot to cook, and anyway it didn't work, so hunting dogs were brought in from the mainland, and the barking and baying drowned out the telly and drove Seán crazy with worry. It took forever until we got control over the situation. Meanwhile, Seán found a rabbit, a kitten of a hare's litter, and snuck it into the house under his sweater. I saw him do it."

"What a sweetheart! Did you say anything?"

"Naw, I wanted to see what would happen. He loved it when Declan and I played along. The three of us were always tormenting our parents."

Toby used to hide behind corners to scare Mom and Anton. Mom would play along, feigning shock after he jumped out, and he laughed so hard his giggles filled the air.

"How long did you keep it hidden?"

"At first, Seán hid it in a shoebox. We fed it leftovers. He'd carry it around in his coat pocket. It survived on milk and cheese, and grass. When Maude and Da were out, we'd let it hop about the house and shake its whiskers. But then it grew without ever getting housebroken. Seán was harboring a wild animal."

"Your parents never knew?"

"One day the rabbit escaped its cardboard crate while we were at school, and chewed through the bottom of a cedar chest that had been in the family for ages. Maude heard the sound and searched for its source. She was arseways. She ruled out everywhere except Seán's room, but there was nothing there, only this maddening noise. She was in a frenzy when we got home, chain-smoking and clutching a rosary, trying to persuade my da to call the priest because she was convinced the house was haunted. 'A dullahan is eating our home, Thomas!' We languished in the yard while my da inspected every inch of the premises. Maude knelt and implored the angels of heaven to shelter us from the storm of malice in the beams and boards. Declan was cracking up the whole time. Seán sat stone silent while our da patrolled the crawlspace, pantry, and closets. Finally he said, 'See? No devils!' Da thought she'd gone mental. He poured himself a beer and opened the newspaper, and that's when Seán lost it and started bawling. Da crouched in front of him, but he wouldn't say a word, just sobbed till his face turned red and his nose ran."

"Poor Seán!"

"Poor Maude! She got it out of him. She poured him his tea and asked why he'd kept it a secret for so long, and he said he didn't want the rabbit to go back to the men with their guns. He didn't want the rabbit to be scared. He was that kind of kid."

"He sounds great."

Tom sat down and patted the deck beside him. I sat, and he pulled me close.

"Can I ask you a serious question? What do you think happens when we die?"

"Do I believe in an afterlife?"

"Yeah."

I called for the chaplain when patients asked me this question. I hadn't thought about it since leaving the States.

"I think I believe in a divine architect, not heaven and hell."

"So you believe in God?"

"Have you seen *The Seventh Seal*?"

"Heard of it."

"It's an old black-and-white movie directed by Ingmar Bergman, from Sweden. A crusader just back from the war meets Death in human form on a beach, and they start talking."

"Death is on the beach? Like sunbathing?"

"Playing chess. So long as the crusader avoids checkmate, he stays alive. During their game, they talk a lot. And in one scene, which I just thought of, they discuss the silence of God."

"He doesn't explain why bad things happen."

"He doesn't stop bad things from happening."

"The problem of evil. What does Death say?"

"Death tells the crusader there may be nothing after death, because God never speaks. But the crusader tells Death there has to be a God. He says something like, 'No man can live with death and know everything is nothing.' In other words, unless there's something after life, nothing during life means anything."

"What do you think?"

"Regardless of after, there's right now."

"I think it's an illusion. All of it."

"It's hard to believe in something after."

"We tell stories to make sense of the world. But they're just stories. We need to make sense of life on our own, without stories."

"If physical death is a certainty, why can't we accept suffering?"

"I don't know. There are so many galaxies out there, we ourselves are very small. I find that comforting."

"How so?"

"Our destruction is insignificant. It means something to us because it's ours, but beyond us, it has no meaning. That's the only thing all strangers have in common. To me it would be a comfort if death were 'lights out,' no more next life, no more this life, just blam! Nothing."

"All of us are essentially the same, but we dwell apart, separated by money, status, and power, things that mean nothing after we die. We don't see one another, and we're lonely because of those same things, since they make us what we are and divide us from ourselves at the same time. Death, for us, is like rain on the ocean. We rejoin each other at our source, all of us the same, no longer distinguishable."

"Or knowable to others, or to ourselves. The peace is in the unknowing."

"Consciousness of self-engenders pain. Our attachments, our egotism, can't serve us in death."

"But in the meantime knowledge is also happiness."

"I wonder. A transient sort of happiness, maybe."

"When I was little, everything was easier. Other people were in charge. My da, for example, he's ten times the sailor I am, and it was a comfort to be in the boat with him when he was steering, I could fully relax so. I could sleep at night without fretting. Now I have to steer."

My father's cortège from St. Clare came back, and I stood under an umbrella watching my uncles shoulder the casket.

"When my dad died I walled myself off to keep from causing conflict in my mother's life. I tried not to make any noise."

"How did it take thirty years for someone like you to show up on my island?"

"What happened to Seán's rabbit?"

"Its name was Sidney. My da built her a hutch in the backyard. She was happy there. Mom left the door open after Seán died, though. Couldn't bear to look at her after."

We sat for a few minutes.

"I'm the one who taught him to swim. It was me. He was decent in the water. As good as a six-year-old could be. I don't usually talk about this."

"I don't mind. What's a date, without a conversation about nothingness?"

"Here's what I needed to tell you. Everyone knows about it, and if you're going to be spending time with me, I should be the one to tell you, so you hear it from me. This happened on a Sunday in April, when the weather was still too cold for swimming, but it was starting to warm up. We hadn't gone to the beach since last September or so, and Seán had been asking. He would walk to da's boat and back, but he knew he wasn't allowed in the water without one of us there. And one day he went in. Or fell in. We don't know. We were all right there, my da on his boat, me on mine, Maude a ways up from us talking to a neighbor. But we weren't watching. He knew the water, knew the dangers. It could have been wind, it could have been play, but whatever it was, he couldn't keep himself up, and he drowned. At first I thought he'd walked back home. I ran up and checked every room. Then there was this frantic walking about, then da and me ran and yelled, then there was Seán, face down in the shallow end, not moving, his shoes still on."

"Was Brigid there?"

"Practically the whole island was there by that point. Their hands to their mouths. Standing silent. Then a helicopter from Galway. Seán had been dead for a while by then, at least half an hour, but Brigid kept administering CPR. My parents went with him on the lift to Galway. I stayed with Declan. He locked himself in his room until our parents came back that night."

Metabolizing death at eight was not what it was in maturity. My memories remained impressionistic and fragmentary, as if I'd gleaned them from someone else's offhand remarks, and I often wondered whether these stories held together by inference had written themselves into my personal history because I'd told and retold them, not because they'd ever taken place, while Tom's memories were those of an adult, solid and real.

"What I can't get out of my head is how cold the water was. I don't want that to be the last thing he felt. I don't want his last moment of life to have been cold. I want it to have been a fire at the hearth. I'm sorry. Excuse me a moment. I'm going to get a bit of air." He stood, opened the door, and stepped outside.

I watched him move into the darkness. I slipped my shoes on and followed him behind the cabin. I took his hand.

"Do you think he felt the cold?"

"In most cases, when someone loses consciousness, they don't feel discomfort or pain."

"I remember little things. He was a fast runner. He was good at math. Listen, Frannie. Here's what I needed to tell you. I had a bad time with it all. I couldn't sleep. I kept going down to the water. Checking where I'd missed him. The Irish say bogs hold the faces of the dead. And I hallucinated. I saw his black hair in the water. I saw it."

I don't know how I knew what was coming next. The way the island tiptoed around Tom. Sidestepped him as though he were cursed. Or protected.

"I don't remember, but Maude came down late one night a week or so after, and found me dressed in land clothes waist deep where he drowned, at the pier where you came ashore on that first day. I was mumbling in the freezing water. Pauly and me da got me out. Brigid came down and sat with me. She had a blanket. That night, she took me to Galway, to the hospital, and I stayed a month there."

I'd seen enough patient intakes to know how awful it was for his parents to think they might lose a second boy.

"That response isn't unusual."

"Have you ever worked in a psych ward?"

"Had a clinical rotation one semester. But that wasn't my specialty."

"What was?"

"Trauma ICU. We had patients who were pretty seriously injured. Car crashes and overdoses."

"Any suicides?"

"We had patients who'd tried."

"It didn't work?"

"Sometimes it worked. Lots of times it didn't, and they'd destroyed their faces and had to breathe through tubes. My preceptor told me I'd get used to it, but I never did. Some things were hard to see. Like my neuro patients. Elevated intracranial pressure, and the external ventricular drains that let off excess cerebrospinal fluid, and sometimes blood. I had to note the color and quantity every hour, very important to do on time. We want our intracranial pressure to be less than twenty-two millimeters after injury. Pupils blown, limbs mangled, punctures from gunshot wounds, organs displaced."

"Jesus, Frannie."

"Sorry. Seeing someone like that gets to you, no matter who they are or how often you see it. My friend assisted patients in a program similar to the one you were in. Treatment for a psychological injury is just as serious as it is for a physical one. Do you remember your time there?"

"I had a view of the bay. Bars on the windows. I remember hands on me in the middle of the night, the first night, almost dawn. I don't know why I remember that. Then they were pushing me through the hallway in a wheelchair. I looked up and saw masks and machines. That first night, I had a roommate I can't remember, another man, who cried a lot, and after a while, I bunked with a second one for a month or so. Then they sent me home. The doctor followed up. They gave me medicine, but it made me feel not like myself, and I quit. I had appointments once a week in Galway, but I didn't go."

"Did you talk with your family?"

"We haven't mentioned it since."

"They have telehealth now if you want to talk."

"Talking won't bring him back. So now you know."

He held me tight. We stayed that way for a long time, leaning against the taffrail.

23

...

Natty Declan, decked out in a tweed cap and olive gilet, cracked eggs on the rim of a skillet.

"You look nice today."

"It's from Cordings. I have to make up for Maude's wardrobe somehow. Plus, tourism season is upon us, and someone's got to set an example. How was the trip? Did you eat the pudding?"

"I did not."

"Was my brother a gentleman?"

"He was."

"So you're pregnant."

"We kissed."

"You made the first move."

"Of course."

"Details, please."

"After work. I swear."

"Tease! You don't want breakfast?"

"Coffee."

"Pregnant for sure. Tell Tommy he'd better not break up with us."

The mornings were growing muggy, and a mist had moved in on the dawn. I cycled uphill to the clinic.

Many of my patients saw island life as drab when compared to the mainland, but the details struck me as extraordinary. The old language they spoke at the pub, the men standing like stones next to their fences, the animals, the scud. I turned by the McAulay farm and pictured myself toiling up the same road in a future time when the past didn't obtrude on the present.

There were no patients. Brigid weeded. I repainted the Gaelic lettering on the sign. The salty breeze smelled like rain.

I heard Tom's voice, and felt his lips, his tongue, his hands. I couldn't help seeing Seán's death, and its effect on the family and community, as something that had happened to Tom, something he'd gone through. A sweet sensation, strangely familiar, often pierced my chest and distracted me, and an unaccustomed openness to the world tempted me away from my tasks at the clinic. On the screen in my head I played and replayed a medium shot of the kiss, as if I were an editor deciding when to cut to a closeup of the frantic look in Tom's eyes at patient intake. Meanwhile Brigid sat by my side and clicked through cell phone plans to find one she could buy for me to use while on call.

I did my clinical rotation in psychiatry at a rehabilitation center on the city's south side. The summer I spent there, the doctors treated a thirteen-year-old who lived in a group home because her mother had lost custody. It would have taken effort for a child that age to become a ward of the state. No doubt she'd endured horror by the time they diagnosed her with borderline personality disorder. She seldom attended group activities. Not one family member came to visit. After a week, she tried to kill herself by eating glass, and they admitted her to the inpatient psychiatric ward.

In her chart I counted eight hospital admissions. The horrid things she blurted startled me at first, but she opened up once we'd spent a little time together. After a group therapy session, she said she didn't want to die, but pain scared her more than death, and she would rather die than live in pain. Having her as a patient caused me to rethink my assumptions about mental health. When every prescription medication failed, they gave her a new diagnosis, refractory Major Depressive Disorder, so that, in a last-ditch effort, they could resort to electroshock therapy, which had come back into practice as a treatment for depression. The option gave her hope. The state declined the request because she had no legal guardian, but we petitioned in court, and after considering her history, the judge approved it. When we told her the good news that night, she looked me in the eye for the first time, and the next morning her gaze was unclouded.

All Tom saw was a bog person, a face in the water, a mask of guilt and grief, a mirror image staring back. Did his nurses think about him? Did they hope he was well? Did he haunt them?

"I'm going to drop the simvastatin at the O'Connor place across the way," Brigid said. "I'll be back before close." I put on the radio and finished her crossword.

Tom Senior and Tom Junior's slip neighbor Felim burst in. A sallow young man shuffled between them, hanging off their arms, face bloodied, head nodding. I steadied him. The wind blew in through the door where I glimpsed two fishermen beside a compact car with a middle-aged woman at the wheel. I guided them to a cot.

"Hold onto him. Call Brigid. I'll take it from here. What's your name?"

"Sam."

"Sam, I'm Frances, the nurse who works with Dr. Neuth. I'm going to look at your forehead now."

I lowered the cot into a reclining position. Blood streaming from between his eyebrows made it difficult to see the injury. Tom Senior and Felim stood at his feet and wrung out their caps.

"Would you gentlemen mind waiting in the other room? I'm going to take good care of you until Dr. Neuth gets here."

His eyes were shut, his heart rate was elevated, his respirations were frequent and short. I shone a light into each eye. Enlarged pupil on the left. Blood pooled at his clavicle. I reached for more gauze and pressed it to his forehead. He had a pair of lacerations, both requiring stitches: one, two inches long at least with a lump beneath it, which could be serious; the other an inch or so.

"Can you tell me about your pain, Sam? On a scale of one to ten. One is mild, ten is intense."

"Two or three. Mueller's donkey kicked me a few years back. That was a kip and a half."

"Brigid's a ways out. She sent a text." Tom Senior showed me his phone:

risk of infection clean and stitch lac

"What medications are you on?"

"I don't take medicine."

"Do you smoke?"

"Yes."

"How frequently?"

"All the time."

"When was the last time you had a cigarette?"

"On the way here."

"How frequently do you drink alcohol?"

"Have you been talking to me ma?"

"Any alcohol today?"

"Not yet."

"Are you allergic to any medication?"

"I don't think so."

I felt around his forehead, gently applied pressure with one hand, and wiped up blood with the other. "Close your eyes for me."

I checked for additional cuts and abrasions. He grimaced. I placed pillows behind his shoulders and prepped the area for stitches.

"You're Tommy's girl, yeah?"

"I suppose I am. You have two lacerations. One above your left eye and one above your left eyebrow. The second cut, thankfully not the one near your eye, is a little deeper than the first. Nothing a few stitches won't fix. We have a lot of blood vessels close to the surface of the skin, and facial wounds often cause quite a bit of bleeding, but it will stop once we apply treatment. Can you tell me what happened today?"

"I can," Tom Senior said.

"I'd like to see if Sam can tell me. But it would help if you wrote down what you remember on that legal pad on the counter, if you don't mind, Tom. I'll use that to fill in Dr. Neuth when she gets back."

"The stay caught me. Stunned me more than anything."

"I'm going to start your stitches now, Sam. First I'll use a shot of lidocaine to numb the area."

"All right."

Sam squinted and gripped the cot. I inserted the needle into the vial.

"What does the stay do? Little sting, here."

"Holds the weight of the mast."

"You're doing great. This side of your face is going to start to feel numb."

I held gauze on the deeper wound, gently felt around the back of his neck, checked his tympanic membrane for blood, and looked in his nose.

"Can you follow my finger?"

He watched my hand move back and forth.

"No blood in your mouth or ears. That's good. Were you knocked out? Any stars or dizziness?"

"Naw."

"Did you get hit anywhere else?"

"Just my gorgeous face. Oh, and my back. Fell on my tailbone."

I rolled him on his side and lifted his shirt. He had a red scratch with some bruising. "Dr. Neuth will take a look at that when she gets here. Can you feel this, Sam?"

I tapped on his forehead.

"Nope."

There were other voices in the waiting room. More men had arrived.

"Are you from Inis Mór?"

"I come from Dingle. My gran left me her property here when she passed. A bunch of grass and two walls. One day I'll build on it."

"That sounds lovely."

"Do you have people here?"

"My dad was from Sligo."

"Good mussels in Sligo."

"Regarding your gorgeous face, any plans to model one day? Maybe for a fishing catalog?"

"I was thinking Rolex or Speedo, like."

"You were hit hard. The stay cut into the top of your dermis. You'll have two small scars after these heal, but your injuries are superficial, and they'll be hard to notice unless someone looks closely."

"Scars are all right. Already covered in them." He lifted his bloody shirt to show a faint line on the lower right abdomen. "Had it out when I was ten with Dr. Brigid, right here."

"Plenty of surface area left for two more, then?"

"You've done this before, right?"

"I have. I did RNFA work in surgery in the States before I moved here. Mostly emergency medicine."

"Deadly. Have you seen gunshot wounds?"

"I have. I'm going to get started now, Sam. Let's have you sit as still as possible. You may feel some pulling, but it shouldn't hurt."

I irrigated the wounds and began the first stitch at the midline of the larger one. He had natural furrows on his brow from being out on the water in the sun. I decided on a pulley closure to conform with his facial muscles.

"You're pretty and nice, at the same time."

"Does it surprise you that your nurse is nice?"

"Girls don't have to be nice if they're good-looking."

"Why not?"

"Don't know. But nice on top of pretty is brilliant. I see why Tommy likes you."

"Thanks, Sam. As still as possible for me, all right?"

"Lucky lad. He can be a right moody git, you know."

"Oh yeah?"

I closed the larger laceration, the one that had knocked him down.

"You all right, Sammy?"

"What happened with the catch?"

"They're bringing up your truck."

"I don't think I could even feckin' count all the scars I've got. There's one on my chest from when I got stuck in a net in Howth, and two on the back of my head from when I fought a bloke outside a chip shop in Dingle. He got me good. That's why I wear my hair long."

"Almost done, Sam."

"Fuck's sake, did all that come out of me?"

"Yep. You had a bleeder."

On the surgical ICU I once saw a patient lose more than a liter of blood. The bleed was coming from someplace in her abdomen. Still, the doctors couldn't determine where, so they turned her hospital bed into an operatory and removed the small bowel to look into the abdominal cavity. At the same time, the resident physician held a flashlight, and I hung two units of blood. And then the tubing cracked and its contents spilled onto the floor. I snatched the bag, sealed it, and cleaned up, but blood had gotten on their hands and inside her. Finally a doctor found a tear in the fascia and threw a stitch in, and the bleeding stopped. Such was emergency care in a major city with a team of doctors and nurses on call. What would happen if a stay hit Tom and he lost consciousness or fell in the water? What if we had to wait for the airlift to Galway? No commercial fishermen wore a life preserver, and they all worked in locations hours away from shore.

I felt Tom's rough palms. He hooked his fingers through the belt loops of my jeans. I closed the second laceration and felt as if, by tending to Sam, I was also caring for Tom, introducing myself to another aspect of Tom's life.

"I like that song. What you were humming just now. 'Dirty Old Town.'"

"I didn't notice I was humming."

"They're one of Tommy's favorites. Came through here once, ages ago, and played mandolin at Maude's."

"All done, Sam."

"Tommy! How in the name of Jesus are ya?"

I turned and saw Tom Junior in his red cap with his Maude, Tom Senior, Felim, and three other men. A few were holding pints.

"Happy hour then?"

"He all right, Frannie?"

"See for yourself."

"You all right then, Sammy?"

"Was a grand auld day until I had to be a dope. Your girl and I were just getting acquainted."

"He'll be fine. He'll be ready to join you in just a few minutes." The newcomers watched me apply betadine to the cuts and cover them with gauze.

"Jesus, he must have lost a pint of blood."

"I'm going to pack a bag with an anti-inflammatory. Sam, I'd like you to stay right there. Tom, will you sit with him?"

Tom sat and patted Sam on the shoulder.

"You got blood on the deck. Looks like a fecking horror movie."

Sam touched the gauze. I collected his medications. The men, having left their work boots outside, surrounded him in thick wool socks.

"It's like a delivery room in here. Who's taking this guy home tonight?"

"I will," said both Toms.

"Is he ready so?"

"We have to wait for Dr. Neuth. She'll be here shortly."

I reviewed aftercare for a distracted Sam, who checked his appearance with his phone's camera. I handed Tommy instructions for the oral medication and cleaning wounds.

"No more hanging around by stays for at least a week. I have one tramadol here, since you bumped your head pretty hard, but I don't want you to take it until you get home for the night. Have you eaten anything recently?"

"Headed to Maude's for her fish fry. Can I buy you a pint?"

"No drink for a few days, Sam. Especially not tonight. Okay? It would be great if you could get that fish to go. I'll take a rain check on that pint."

"I mean it, Frances. Thanks a million."

His eye had already swelled shut. I handed him an icepack.

"It was my pleasure. Who do you stay with, Sam?"

"No wife, but I'm in love with you, on account of you saving my life. And my face."

He winked with his other eye.

"He can stay on my couch," Tom Junior said.

"I was only coddin' ya!"

The bell on the door announced Brigid's arrival. She examined Sam's face.

"Well done, Frances. And you, sir! What's happened now?"

"Doc, I can explain!"

"Frances, did you go over aftercare?"

"She did."

"Any nausea?"

"Naw."

I added to Sam's chart, noting the details of the procedure and a possible follow-up in Galway. I was glad the injury hadn't been more serious. What would an emergency have been like on the island? For a moment I missed the resources of the hospital.

"Keep your face clean, new bandage once a day. We may need to talk about a CT, but you're fine for tonight. What's this about bruising your back?"

She snapped the curtain shut.

Tom Junior watched me from across the room. His beard was coming in a little red.

"You're pure class, you know that?"

I clicked and typed and smiled. Watching him watch me was like stealing glances between lines of the Homily.

"I can't stop thinking about last night."

"You and me both."

"Can I see you later on? I'll get Sam settled first."

"For sure."

Brigid opened the curtain.

"Tommy, let's have a hand here."

Tom held Sam up, and Brigid followed with a stream of instructions.

How easily they trusted each other. Proximity and consistency. They watched each other day after day, as they all remained the way they'd been, or changed into someone else. I'd never stayed anywhere long enough. In the city, anonymity forced a sort of involuntary independence. I'd become a part of their world. A newer fixture, but a fixture nonetheless.

An ancient truck idled. Tom Junior and two other men climbed in the bed on either side of Sam. A cloud of exhaust.

"I'll be by Maude's in a bit, gorgeous," Tom said. Sam kissed the air and sang, "I'll be your true love forever." The rest joined in and sputtered down the road.

"Tell me you aren't ever leaving this island," Brigid said.

I watched the truck move off toward the pier.

"You couldn't pay me to."

24

...

Clouds hung low, and no rain fell, but the wind picked up and brought a brief early summer chill to the work that kept me at the clinic until long after business hours.

Doolin Express ferries pulled in throughout the day at Kilronan pier, where minivans transported passengers to Dún Aonghasa, then back to the pubs. Declan worked eighteen-hour days. My ride to the clinic now took me through European holiday traffic, slow rented bikes on a gusty hill road. Wanda rented her other room to a German family who came into the clinic with nausea as soon as the ferry landed. After my shift I heard their voices through the walls. Tourists stopped me for directions, twice.

Scrapes, concussions, flu, back spasms, upper respiratory infections, chest pains, and regularly scheduled check-ups and vaccinations kept the clinic busy. Tom was away most nights till sunset, nearly nine o'clock.

Fatigue had set in by nightfall, and we all slumped over in the pub, where live music lulled us as we ate and drank. Tom and I met late and got a pint at Maude's. If he returned past closing time, he'd stop by my room and teach me to make a fire. One windy Friday night, he carried in a cord of firewood, and we tiptoed to the bed and made out to the sound of Wanda's voice on the phone, and fell asleep with the lights on.

With Tom's body beside mine I slept soundly for the first time in years. The daily rushes of reality played in my dreams instead of the horror prequel I'd left behind. Normalcy precludes nightly social calls from your murder victim.

One morning I rose before dawn. Grey streaks of rain distorted the pier. Michael Collins slept in front of the fire. I watched Tom. I wondered when we would make love. Our time together was hasty and haphazard, and we were constantly under the scrutiny of islanders who seemed to know something we didn't.

I set down a cup of tea beside the bed.

"Tommy."

I laid a hand on his chest.

"What time is it?"

"Five o'clock. I brought your tea."

"Shite, I'm sorry."

"Not exactly sailing weather."

"How come you're up so early?"

"A fisherman was in my bed."

"The bastard. Where is he?"

His phone buzzed. Thunder shook the windows.

"Let me check that."

"Is anyone going out?"

"Apparently not. But me da is with Pauly in the shop. His fuel pump is shot to hell."

"Five more minutes. We can take in the sunrise."

"Grand."

I closed my eyes. Rain pelted the glass.

The next day I called my mom. She asked how work was going and whether I'd be back for Christmas. Between our distant words I heard dishes being washed and stacked. She offered to visit. I told her I'd love that.

"You're happy?"

"I am."

"I miss you."

"I miss you guys too."

"Think you'll visit Sligo?"

"I don't know yet."

"You're so close to where he spent nearly his whole life."

"I think about that too."

"Do your friends know about him?"

"Some."

"It's nice to think of you there."

Every part of me ached by the time my alarm went off on Friday morning. I lingered looking at the vista of boats outlined against the sky, a tableau that was transforming itself before my eyes with the changing of the seasons, from louring Low Country seascape gray to dazzling Midi blue. I ran my hands along the sheet where Tom had lain. The night before was the closest we'd come to making love. Talking, then touching, but without our habitual reserve. We were nearly naked when three raps on my door interrupted us.

"Frances, you awake?"

It was Wanda.

"One second."

I got dressed and slipped out.

Her daughter Colleen had a nosebleed, a gusher, as she called it, and I followed her into the main house, to find the girl staring down at a blood-soaked pajama top.

I returned to an empty room, Tom long offshore, and found a note by last night's fire:

Come to dinner tonight? The boat at 7. Tommy

I put the kettle on, dressed for work, and tucked the scrap of paper in my jeans.

Newcomers sat in locals' seats at the pub, Wormhole divers, glampers, honeymooners, and day trippers, few, thankfully, American.

One day, without a word from anyone, no document or stamp, I woke to find I'd drifted from the status of visitor to that of resident, and I'd become Tom's girlfriend and he my boyfriend, silently acknowledged as such by the islanders. Welterweights of love. I'd bring him his tea, he'd build my fire. I worried about him on the boat; he walked me home at night.

Once, when I'd ducked under Wanda's awning in a downpour and huddled with my chest to the wall, he pressed himself against my back, held my wrists, caressed my jaw, and kissed the nape of my neck; during this moment and others like it, being restrained under Tom's control intensified and prolonged the shiver of desire that ran through me, and his tenderness reassured me he wouldn't do what Anton had done. He whispered, "I could drink rain from your skin forever."

I sometimes wondered whether, for the sake of my professional relationship with the community, and out of deference to the islanders' affection for Tom, we should have kept our relationship a secret, and avoided the eyes of gossips. I was an outsider, after all.

I worried about what I hadn't told him. Would he need to find out? Would someone look me up and find a headline from two years before?

He was easygoing and patient, I noticed while observing him with the other fishermen, as well as soft-spoken, temperate, selective in the company he kept, and loyal to his family. His friends seemed like good men. He never once commented on Dad's ashes.

I rode my bike up the windy hill, stopping at the McAulay's, whose donkey lumbered over, bell clanking. I waved to Birdie McAulay, in her house dress, hanging laundry on the line beside her clachan. She waved and hobbled to the fence.

"Hello, Birdie."

"Howya, Frances! Maureen waits for you every day."

"Maureen?"

"Maureen O'Hara, dear."

Maureen O'Hara ate her apple.

"How are those knees?"

We'd given Birdie cortisone injections the week before.

"The young don't know what age is. One second, dear."

She limped to her mailbox and handed me some papers handwritten in Irish.

"Will you give these to Maude at the pub tonight?"

"Sure thing, Birdie. What does it say? I can't read Gaelic."

"I need some help. Ryegrass Maureen can't manage. And my lace wall is crumbling. Some things inside too."

"We'll all help out."

"I'm about ready to sell. Trade it for a pint of gat, I would. I'm getting on in years. The upkeep gets harder and harder."

"I'll give these to Maude."

"I'm not looking to put anyone out."

"I'll tell Tom Archer about the wall. He and Declan could get that fixed up in an afternoon."

"Agh, Miss Frances!"

"It wouldn't be any trouble. The Archer boys have strong backs."

"That's true, and your Tommy is always following about. Come to think of it, I could use those boys for carrying my peat. Bring them by in the grand stretch with you. Just let me know the day. I'll make a colcannon."

"I'll do that."

"You're a good girl yourself, Frances. Why don't you settle down here with us?"

"That's the plan. Just need to save to get a lot of land. Know of anyone looking to sell?"

"All of us. Kelly, my youngest, is in Mayo. She's offered me her guest room."

"Wouldn't you miss the island?"

"Better to be closer to the hospital. And to family."

"Makes sense. The moment you decide to sell, you've got a buyer. I'll be by after work tomorrow to help you a bit inside."

The day passed slowly as I anticipated a second night with Tom. Dinner sounded formal, but his boat would be more private than our rooms. To purchase contraceptives would be to broadcast our intimacy to the villagers. Would they watch me board his boat? Would he cook elsewhere and bring the meal aboard? I'd seen his apartment once, cramped quarters with a single window, a couch last upholstered before the Easter Rising, more like a hostel than a home.

We had two patients, one with a sore throat, the other with an impacted splinter. I left early, showered, and sat at Maude's to wait for Tom with a cup of Barry's and my sketchbook.

Old timers discussed their catch, teens tuned instruments. Through the open window next to the fireplace, a horse pulled a cart past a crowd of tourists.

Tom Senior stiffly stretched and poured himself a cup of tea.

"Hiya, Frances. What do you have there? Pauly, then! That's nice. You're generous with that pencil of yours. He's never looked better. Do me next, when I'm not expecting it. What do you charge?"

"For you? No cost."

"Pauly, come look. She got you at your good angle."

Pauly looked up and came over. He had thick salt and pepper sideburns and carried a cold pipe. I recognized him from Sam's clinic visit.

"Will you look at that. Can I have it for my wife? I've never looked better."

"That's what I said."

"How much?"

"No charge. You're an excellent subject."

I handed him the sketch.

"Don't forget to sign it. I learned that from watching *The Works*. Doesn't count with no signature."

I signed, and Pauly folded it into his coat pocket.

"Tom, a pint for the lady."

"Not a problem. Did you pull in that velvet catch?"

"Gorgeous haul."

"I'll have a Barry's. What's velvet?"

"Fiddlers," Pauly said.

"Here, I'll show you," Tom Senior said. He scrolled on his phone.

"You can do better than that, High Hook. Show her the live well, Tommy."

Tom's hair was still wet from the shower. It had grown longer since I met him, and showed a cowlick in the front that gave him an unkempt look.

"That's what's for dinner, so."

He kissed me on the forehead. Tom Senior, eyes warm on Tom Junior, sipped his tea.

"She's your girl, then?"

"I don't cook crab for just anyone."

"Maude is making crab cornbread tonight," Tom Senior said. "Shall we get the haul?"

"Want to see dinner in its live form?" Tommy asked.

We trailed Pauly and Tom Senior to the pier. Tom took a bottle of screw top wine from the storeroom. The other two walked with pints of stout. The dockies were wrapping up. Michael Collins brought up the rear.

"It's quiet out there."

"Look at those low clouds moving in from the west. Won't be still for long."

"How was yours today, Pauly?" Tom Senior asked.

"No cod. Only pollock. You been out with Tommy yet, Miss Frances?"

"Not yet. How do you find the best spots?"

"We mark the schools on our sonars. Bigger the fish, bigger the pay. And by the way, tonight's a special occasion. Maude makes the best crab along the whole coast, so we're keeping a bushel."

"Declan would like a word," Tom Junior said.

"How many do you get in a day?"

"Goal is a couple hundred pounds. Jumbos pay almost three times what the smaller ones bring."

"And they're kept alive until you sell them?"

"Some. We hold them in the salt water or sit them on ice."

"Best market is in Galway Bay. Close to where Tommy went to school," Tom Senior said.

Tom's boat was tied in a slip next to twenty other smaller commercial boats. It was newer than his father's, white with a blue stripe, with a higher and narrower captain's bridge. Pauly and Tom Senior walked across the slip toward Tom Senior's boat. Michael Collins panted near the dock and darted over when Tom whistled to lift and put him down on the deck. Tom Senior and Pauly loaded one last heavy basket from a bait tank. Tom put a hand out and helped me up. The first raindrops fell.

"Here you go then, love. Sea can sometimes be still. Especially just before the storm."

Tom unlocked his own bait tank and showed me dozens of fish swimming around. A lightning bolt lit the sky.

"Best get inside," Pauly hollered. He and Tom Senior lugged a bucket of crab up the hill toward Maude's. Then it started to rain.

"It's pissing down," Tom said, "And you don't have a jacket."

I followed him to the bridge. He unlocked the cabin.

A head and a berth. There were changes of clothes, a few paperbacks, bars of soap in boxes, and bottles of water. Tom led me in and flipped on the lights. There were walkies and radios, a knife, sunglasses, fishing test, an unused ashtray, a bag of apples, and a coffee cup filled with pencils and decorated with pink roses and ANDREW in cursive. A bobble hula dancer gyrated above his navigational materials.

"This is the helm. Where the magic happens." I sat on a bench across from the captain's seat and smoothed my wet hair. "I've had this boat since my twenty-second birthday. It was a gift from Tom and Maude."

"Is this where you bring all your dates?"

"Just the lucky ones."

He gave me a towel from his cabinet and switched on a small propane heater in the corner. The thermos he'd shared with me the day we met sat next to the steering wheel. I recognized the clothes in the small closet. There were old newspapers, boxes of Barry's, rolls of jute twine, and tattered paperbacks, among them a volume of selected poems by Ted Hughes along with an old spiral notebook that had his handwriting on the cover.

"Shall we open this?"

"Like civilized Irish, we will drink from my cabin stemware."

He fetched the tumbler and a coffee cup.

The CB cracked. He leaned across me to pick it up.

"Tommy."

"Just checking on youse."

"Yeah, fine. You all inside all right?"

"Yep. It's lashing down. Wait to onboard. Pauly slipped twice."

"Rotten out. You get the crab in okay?"

"Aye"

"All right, Pop, over."

"Over."

"Your folks check up on you like mine do?"

"It's their job to worry."

"Do you like Ted Hughes?"

"I don't know him."

"English Poet Laureate. Died a few years back. Wrote a lot about the wildlife on the moors. Married to an American, Sylvia Plath. You ever read her?"

"I read *The Bell Jar* in school. Pretty tragic stuff. What made you get into poetry?"

"Don't know if I'd say I'm into it. Never published anything."

"Your Mom said you were good with words."

He sat close beside me. "How come Maude is telling you all my secrets?"

"I think you should read me something you've written."

"Oh, Jesus. Come here to me first."

"It's all right if you're shy."

"I've never shown a girl anything I've written."

"Seeing your writing can only increase my affection."

"All right, you can read one, but I get to choose." He picked up the notebook.

"You've navigated storms, and you're nervous about a poem?"

"I'd take a storm over this."

He handed me the notebook. The handwriting was the same as the annotations.

Stockholm Syndrome

How hard it is to put your thumb on a feeling, said
    the gull,
How peculiar, it's like slowly growing attached to
    someone,
As when I sailed to you for the first time—you with
    your lonely charm
And provincial good manners—from yet another
    port in the sea,
Said the gull, just another stop along Na Cealla
    Beaga.

Sailing home, kidnapped, scowling, my poetry back
    then was a match
I played against myself on a pitch of rocks and dust,
    always wanting to compete
In the Premier Division on bright green grass instead,
Not thrashing, seasick, offshore, like a pianist
    touching keys too out of tune
For the chords to ring out perfectly on the breath.

Now winter has come once more, a pearlescent sky
    rolls in,
Only a few thousand casts of my line and I'll be
    gone.
We never played the same song, our fires never
    burned as one,
But after each of those mornings with you on the
    outskirts, said the gull,
Your shoulder pushing into mine, some part of me
    missed you.

"How long ago did you write this?"
"Last January. About Killybegs. Old fishing town in Donegal.
Good for Gaelic football."

He stood, cupped his hands against the window, and peered out.

"I need to check the ties."

"Can I keep reading?"

"Sure."

He ducked out.

I flipped through the notebook. Scribbled notes, lists, lines crossed out, newspaper clippings, receipts, a ticket stub from a Galway club. Pasted on one page was a cutout of an old woman, beside a poem:

An Cailleach

A fisherman waits tensely for the touch
of airy fingers on the line
    and hears the low whistle of a keening song
    balk at the currach

and scans the shore for a finger
of smoke and steers beneath clouds dark as waves.
    Thunder cracks the sky into strands.
    Rain pounds the boat

and island people are intimate with water yet
An Cailleach is the mother of the storm
    whose reign is winter and whose realm is grief.
    The fisherman crosses himself.

On a sod roof old An Cailleach stirs
up from seaweed and apple cores left to rot,
    skin like peat, leaves in her hair,
    one eye to know the world by.

He came back in.

"Boat is fine. Ties are sound. Best stay put for a bit. Looks as though you're stuck here with me and Michael Collins."

"You don't seem the least bit troubled by inclement weather. Do the storms ever worry you? "

"We're just as safe here as we would be on land. Nights I don't stay on the boat I fall asleep to BBC's Shipping Forecast."

"You listen to a weather channel?"

"Fisherman's lullaby."

He leaned in and kissed me. I tasted wine on his lips.

"Speaking of storms, how do you say this?"

"An Cailleach."

"What is it?"

"Sea goddess. Old Irish myth. She rules over tempests and winter. You're soaked."

"My Archer sweater has water in it."

"You should enquire about a return."

"I'll take this up with the manager's son."

He caressed my face, kissed my lips, and neck. He reached inside my bra and touched my breast, licked my nipple, stubble against my skin. His mouth moved to my belly, his hands lower. He kissed my hip bones and tucked his hand inside the seat of my jeans. I pulled off my sweater and knelt before him in just my soaked bra. He pulled me against him and lifted my leg around his waist. He unbuttoned my jeans. I stopped his hand.

"I want you," I said. "But I want the moment to feel right. And I don't have protection."

"In that case, I'm unprepared too. I was getting ahead of myself there."

"So was I."

"How do we decide if a moment is right? Assuming we have protection. I've never thought about it. I just went through the motions, I guess."

"How come you didn't make the first move on Inis Oírr?"

"Being close to you felt like holding onto sand. I had to be cautious. I couldn't let it slip through my fingers or make any mistakes."

"What mistakes?"

"Rushing. Fumbling. I wanted you to feel how serious I was."

"I've been pining for you since I saw you on the boat ride over."

"While you were puking?"

"Yeah, when we caught each other's eye."

"Meant to mention, thanks for saving Sam. He's a fan."

"How's he feeling? He never called us to follow up."

"And never will. If my da hadn't forced him to the clinic, he'd have patched up his face with a poultice of tape and caulk. Will I get to meet your people?"

"They're far away."

"You don't talk about them."

"Not much to tell."

He took a slow breath. "It feels like you're hiding. Like you put up a wall whenever I ask about where you're from."

"You didn't scare me off on your Dad's boat. I hope I don't scare you off on yours. Remember when we went swimming and you asked if I was on the run?"

"A man?"

"Dead man."

"Husband?"

"Stepfather."

"Dead, how?"

"Because of me."

"What happened?"

"One night my mom called me. He hadn't come home after work. They fought all the time, so I was used to calls like that. But this time, she sounded different."

"Different how?"

"It was payday. She was worried about money. I knew where he was. He spent a lot of nights at Baby's, this tavern around the corner from their place. So I decided to talk to him. Toby followed me, the little man of the house. I went in. Anton was sitting there and I opened his wallet and took out a stack of twenties."

"Look at you. Not afraid to have a go."

"He was drunk. He saw Toby a few feet behind me. I told him he should be ashamed of himself. Then I said, 'Shame on you for serving him,' to the bartender. Then I walked out and took Toby with me."

"Where did you go?"

"Back to my mom's."

"How long had it been since your Dad passed?"

"Long time. I was eight."

"When did she meet the next bloke?"

"Few years after. They met at work."

"Sounds like a pox. You two ever get on?"

"He never liked me."

"Go on."

"The nights he drank, he rarely came home. I don't know where he stayed. If my mom knew, she never said. If he came home, he'd complain, pick fights, get handsy with mom. That night I slept on the couch. I don't know what I thought that would accomplish. We thought the lock would keep him out. At one o'clock, we heard his steps. Then he was pounding on the mudroom door. He broke the chain. The police took pictures of the damage the next day. Mom ran out of her room. Anton was on top of her, hollering about me and Toby embarrassing him at Baby's. Toby came out of his room. Anton called me a thief and said I wasn't raised right. I saw the neighbors' lights go on. Mom put her hand on his chest, and he slapped her. Then Toby hit him and yelled. Mom was crying. I got in between them. He punched me with a right hook, and my head hit the table. I was out for a minute. My vision was fuzzy. I looked up and saw the big beam that ran across the ceiling. The room spun and spun, and then Anton was on top of Toby, and he had his knee on Toby's chest, and he called him a little shit. Toby was crying. Mom was trying to pry Anton off, but he didn't budge. I saw the stack of garden pots in the corner by the door. I grabbed the biggest one. Toby's eyes were glassy. I hit Anton on the head. Toby scrambled away, coughing and gasping. Anton fell over on his side. Blood was coming from his head and soaking into the carpet. He got up on his hands and knees. He touched his head and looked down at his hand.

Toby's baseball gear was next to the couch. I grabbed one of the bats and got ready to swing if he took another step. Anton called me a thieving bitch. Blood was dripping down his face. He said he was going to teach me a lesson. I said the police were on the way. He steadied himself against the wall. Then he left. Mom took charge for once and drove us to the police station. She said she was sorry, and this time we were leaving. Toby sat with me in the back seat.

There was a young cop at the front desk. He gave me a yellow legal pad and told me to write down what happened. Which took forever because my hands were shaking and I could only open one eye. I could see Mom and Toby through the glass. The officer read what I'd written. He kept clicking his pen while I stared at my eye in a Styrofoam cup of black coffee. Then he took the pad and went down the hall and talked to another cop who was sitting on the edge of a desk with papers all over it. Then the first cop came back with a new bag of ice wrapped in a brown paper towel, and we left for the hospital."

"Were you hurt?"

"Concussion. Black eye for a week. Could have been worse."

"Toby?"

"Had to have a CT once we moved to Mercy, but he was clear. His injuries were more psychological."

"Where did Anton go?"

"We went from the police station to the hospital by ambulance. Mom stayed with Toby in his room. I was in my own room next door. An officer stood guard outside."

"Did Anton come back?"

"No."

I took a long look at Tom's face and considered the likelihood that we might never see eye-to-eye again after he heard what I was about to say.

"We asked for a police escort home to make sure Anton wasn't there. But the officer said it wouldn't be necessary. They told us

Anton wouldn't be coming back. They got him. They found him lying by the curb on Franklin a few blocks from the house. He was dead."

"Good feckin' riddance. I'd wring his neck myself if the bastard weren't already dead. I'm sorry you had to go through all that."

"I thought I should tell you what I did before we got closer."

"What you did was save your brother. This cunt had it coming. Anyway it was self-defense. Was the blow the cause of death?"

"No other sign of injury."

"Don't you be sorry. You've got what soldiers have after war. Were you supposed to sit there and watch? You were defending your family. Did you leave the States because of that? Is that why you're here?"

"Yeah. Afterwards I always felt like people were watching me everywhere I went, and they knew what had happened to my family."

"But you were cleared. No arrest."

"All clear."

Camera flash as I show my injury. Grain of the wood table as I'm deposed. Questions. Courtroom echo.

"But it's still inside there, yeah?"

"The longer I stayed, the colder everything felt. So I took off."

"To Inis Mór."

"I was scared to tell you. I didn't want to lose my chance with you."

"Lose me?"

He put his arm around my shoulder. I curled up against him and laid a hand on his heart. He covered my hand with his. The boat was still, the cabin quiet, except for the bush crickets that sang in the pier's salty grasses.

"What do you want most?" he asked.

"Trust."

"That'd be grand."

"Does the noise of the tide ever frighten you?"

"Just earth and moon breathing together. I've got you."

He kissed my forehead. I leaned against him. He slipped his hands beneath my sweater. We sat that way until exhaustion caught up with us and we struggled to keep our eyes open.

Tom fell asleep first. I lay watching him in the half-light. I closed my eyes and waited, and did not dream.

We woke to a pecking gull. Men moved about the pier, voices muted. Michael Collins lay on a coil of rope. Tom stretched.

"Do you need to go?"

"I work at nine."

"Twelve past five. I'm not ready to let go of you just yet."

An engine started. I smelled pipe tobacco. Michael Collins scratched at the door.

"We should get up."

"Want to take in the sunrise? I'll walk you home."

"Think you can get me back without anyone seeing us?"

"Not a chance. It's already in the morning paper."

"What about your mom?"

"She's been pushing me to ask you out since the first day you got here. I knew when she offered you our sweater."

"Really?"

"It was the least she could do. She caught you staring."

"You were eating that brown bread. I was starving."

"I'm starved now. Let's go for breakfast. I know a place."

"Why do we always make out on boats?"

"Let me show you the many advantages of the ocean over land."

Two slips over, the old timer Felim, with a pipe in one hand and a bucket in the other, gaped as I stepped down from Tom's boat.

"Morning."

Felim tipped his hat. Tom and I climbed the hill to my room, and he took my hand.

"So I'm your fella."

"Only if Michael Collins is part of the deal."

"Agreed."

Wanda and her two kids stopped in the row, looked at us, and moved on.

"I only stay over on fishing boats during inclement weather if I'm smitten."

"I can't have Felim asking after you in the pub now, can I? I'd have to ask him to step outside."

...

25

Two mornings later, I woke to raps on my door an hour before my alarm was set to go off. Two islanders spoke into cell phones next to Maude in the walkway outside.

"Brigid just rang," Maude said, and handed me her phone. Wanda stood by in a bathrobe.

"Hello, Brigid?"

"Frances, we have to get you a cell phone."

"What's going on?"

"Sixty-year-old female, west side of the island. Her husband thinks she's broken her leg."

"Do you want me to stay at the clinic or go along with you?"

"I just closed it for the day. I need you with me in case we call for an airlift. Can you be ready to go in ten minutes?"

"Yes. See you outside Maude's."

I changed into warm clothes and brushed my teeth. I locked my door and walked to Maude's, and Brigid pulled up in her husband's car.

"It'll be a quick trip. Tom Senior will go along in case she needs to be moved."

"Let's go," Tom Senior said. Tom Junior stepped into Maude's. I stuck my head in the door.

"I'll come find you when I'm back?"

"I'm going too," he said, and put his cap on.

The car climbed the bumpy road to the interior of the island. Brigid briefed me.

"Sixty-two-year-old woman, currently prescribed Prinivil and Trexall. Not a fall risk. Must have been an accident on the property. Right leg isn't weight-bearing. She's conscious, but her husband said she appears 'stunned.' Possible concussion."

I filled out the intake forms on her iPad.

"What did you bring for pain?"

"Oxycodone to start. I can't administer anesthesia without the airlift. They're waiting for our call. Tonight, we will get you a phone. Here's Sloan's until it comes."

"You took your daughter's phone?"

"I gave her life. She understands."

We parked beside a flat white house with a sea view that I'd cycled past a dozen times. Brigid popped the trunk. The men collected her equipment.

"Surprised Tommy came along," she said.

"What do you mean?"

"He knows the O'Briens, is all."

"Who are they?"

"His ex-fiancée's family."

An older gentleman in a herringbone newsboy hat paced at the start of a narrow driveway.

"Thanks for comin'," he said, reaching an arthritic hand for mine.

We climbed the steep hill to a row of cottages, then followed him inside one, and down a hallway to a small bedroom with the shades drawn. Phyllis lay on her side.

"Hiya, Phyllis," Brigid said. "So sorry to hear you've had a fall. This is Frances White, a nurse who's at the clinic with me now. Can you tell me about your fall?"

"When I got up yesterday, I felt this little tug in my right leg."

"Here, or higher, here?"

"Higher," she answered. "And as I walked around during the day, I felt an ache. It didn't go away when I sat. I thought it was arthritis. Before I fell, I couldn't move my leg. Why is that?"

I added all of this to her forms on the iPad. I could hear Tommy and Tom Senior shuffling around in the other room.

"Your hip is a ball-and-socket joint. Its structure allows the leg to move in all directions. If that joint is compromised, it could be the cause of those symptoms. Tell us about the fall."

"I was walking in the garden and my leg buckled."

"Did you feel any dizziness?"

"No."

"We're going to look at you a little more closely. Can you lie on your back for me now?"

I shone a light into Phyllis' eyes.

"Phyllis, I am going to ask you some questions. Could you please answer either yes or no?"

"Yea."

"Any loss of consciousness since you fell?"

"No."

"Having a hard time staying awake?"

"I don't think so."

"Any nausea or vomiting?"

"No."

"Headache?"

"Just a hip ache."

"Any pain in your neck?"

"No."

"Any loss of vision or double vision?"

"No."

"Tingling or weakness in your arms or legs?"

"Yes, my leg."

"Which leg?"

"My right."

Brigid palpated around her hip and lower back for swelling, looking for bruising patterns or vascular injury. "Tell me when you feel any pain, Phyllis," she said. "Frances, the popliteal."

"Fifty in the right leg."

"Left?"

"Eighty."

"Wiggle your toes again in your left leg, Phyllis. Now you're right. And have you put weight on it?"

"I tried. It hurt too badly."

Brigid moved the right joint a bit, and Phyllis winced.

"Is it broken?"

"I can't tell that without an X-ray. I'm seeing a bit of joint abnormality. Your injured leg is a bit shorter than the other leg, and you can't put any weight on it. This could be an issue with your pelvis, but we don't know until we can get you to Galway."

"Oh, God."

"These things happen. Frances is going to get you comfortable. I'm going to just call the hospital."

Brigid stepped into the hallway.

"I don't want to be a trouble."

"It's no trouble to get you well. I have some pain medication here that will help you feel more comfortable. Do you have any allergies, Phyllis?"

"Cats."

"This is ten milligrams of Oxycodone."

"Christ, what's that?"

"It's a pain medication Brigid has prescribed for you. Works quickly to help you feel better. I'd like you to eat a little something with it. Have you had breakfast?"

"Nothing yet today."

"Tom, can you please find me something small for Phyllis to eat? Some crackers, maybe?"

He nodded and disappeared.

"Do you think it's broken?"

"Only an X-ray can confirm that, but even if it is, these breaks are treatable."

"Do you think I'll be an invalid?"

"I don't suspect you'll be an invalid. I'm going to apply a topical lidocaine patch as well."

"I'll take anything that helps."

"Let's have you lie still for me. You'll start to feel better in just a minute here."

"So you're American then?"

"I am. I'm from the Midwest."

"Oh, I always wanted to go to San Francisco. I've heard it's just grand."

"When this hip heals up, you should treat yourself with a trip over."

"Maybe."

Brigid came back in, pocketing her phone.

"Lidocaine patch and ten milligrams of Oxycodone," I said.

"All right, Mrs. O'Brien," Brigid said. "No moving from that bed, you hear?"

"Does it look like I'd be capable of moving, Brigid? Look at the state of me. I'm practically an invalid."

The airlift from University Hospital arrived. The flight nurse, a stocky man named Gavin, hopped off the helicopter. Most flight nurses back at the ICU had seen combat. They were brave and strong. I couldn't make it on a ferry, let alone fly in blackout. I ducked under the rotors and greeted him.

"New in town?" Gavin said.

"That obvious?"

"You here permanently?"

"For now."

"Suppose this is a change of pace."

"I'd take this over trauma ICU any day."

Brigid and Gavin moved Phyllis into the back of the helicopter. Brigid hopped in to help secure her as the pilot reviewed the instructions.

"That Tommy Archer?"

"Yeah."

"Will you tell Tommy's brother Declan that Gavin sends his regards?"

"Sure thing. He a friend of yours?"

"He comes by the station whenever he's in Galway. He's teaching me to cook. We've been encouraging him to try out for *The Great British Bake-Off* for four seasons now."

"He'd sweep it!"

"Tell him to give me a call when he's next over."

"I'll do that."

"Cheers!"

Brigid shook hands with Gavin, and he closed the door between us. We stepped back, watched the helicopter take off.

It was nearly evening by the time we arrived back at Maude's. Brigid chattered. I kept my head down in the back seat beside

Tom, who looked out the window. Outside Maude's, Brigid and I hugged, and she drove off.

"You haven't eaten at all today, Frances," Tom Senior said, pushing open the door to Maude's. "I'm famished. You must be too."

I heard her voice, shrieking "Thomas Archer!" before I saw her. Then a slight blonde embraced Tom, a stony recognition on his face. He stood between us, but I guessed this was the former fiancée. She looked him over. He put an arm around her, as he had around me the night before.

"Hiya Susan," Tom said. I joined Sam at the bar. Declan looked from Tom to me.

"How's she cuttin', Frannie?" Sam asked, his healing eye taut pink in the pub's lights. "Crab is good tonight. So that's the ex."

"I figured."

Her voice drew nearer.

"Sure look," Declan said to Sam, who rolled his eyes.

"Hiya, Declan," Susan chirped.

"I will, yeah," Declan sighed and walked to the other end of the bar.

I turned and saw Susan take Tom's arm as he stood with his hands stuffed in his pockets, appearing as if he might throw up on the floor in front of all of us. He looked everywhere but at me.

"So, you're Brigid's little helper," Susan said.

"Frannie, this is Susan. You took care of her ma today."

"Nice to meet you," I said.

Her black eyes leveled on mine. "Thanks so much for taking care of me ma. She said you were just the sweetest! I've been hearing all about you."

"Happy to help."

"Fuck's sake," Sam said. He laughed and passed me the newspaper.

"I came as soon as I heard," Susan said. "I'm headed to Uni Hospital first thing tomorrow. And wasn't it so sweet of Thomas to go all that way too?"

She gazed at Tommy.

"Yeah. Tom's a real softie," Sam jabbed. Tom shot him a look. I opened the paper and stirred my tea.

"Ma always loved you, didn't she?"

Susan draped her arms around Tom.

"Back in a minute," Tom said. He slid out of Susan's grip.

"How are you getting on, Sammy?" Susan asked. "Where's the craic around here? You're hardly in it."

Sam nodded, eyes on the television.

"So, you're American?" Susan asked. She stood about six inches from my face. She was wearing high heels. "How come you're out here with all these culchies?"

"This geebag calls us culchies, and she grew up down the way," Sam said.

"Feck off."

Michael Collins sniffed between our feet.

"Ugh, why do you always let your dog in here? Isn't it a Department of Health violation or something?"

She gave Michael Collins a rough scoot. He yelped and scurried off.

"I was going to say, you have to be American. You don't look Irish at all. What part of America do you come from?"

"New York."

She looked me up and down.

"She is Irish, you dope," Sam said. "Her people are from Sligo."

"Eew, a coal town."

"Frances, come on down here," Sam said, patting the empty stool to his right. I joined him. Susan followed.

"What brings you to our little island?"

"Work."

"I'm in marketing," she said. "I work an hour outside London, but I'm hoping to find something in the city within the year. I just love the vibe. Why would you want to work here when you could be somewhere that's actually happening?"

"How's the eye, Sam?"

"Right as rain. Look okay to you?"

"Just a little granulation. Totally normal. You're healing nicely."

"Thanks a million."

"Look at you two. Adorable. Americans love our little island, don't they, Sam?"

"For fuck's sake."

"You and Thomas love this time of year, yeah? All the girls here on holiday. Best beware, what's your name again?"

"Frances."

"Best beware, Frances. These boys have a reputation."

"Will you feck off, Susan?" Sam said. Declan looked over from where he stood. Tom came around the corner carrying dinner.

"Have Sam tell you about the ladies' diving team that came through a few years back. These boys rode up to the Wormhole every afternoon to make their catch."

Tom set down the dinner plates.

"Made some new friends, didn't you, Thomas?"

"Susan's having a grand time telling us about your priors," Sam said. "You're awfully thick with that mouth."

"I'm only teasing, ya big dope. Thomas, tell yer man to relax."

I excused myself. In the bathroom I threw water on my face and scrutinized it in the mirror. I heard the click of high heels as I turned off the faucet.

"How are ya, Frances?"

She leaned against the basin and grinned.

"It's all yours."

"No, wait a second. Just wanted a word in private."

"What is it?"

"I know it must be hard, seeing the ex and all."

"We all have our pasts."

"Oh, and he does have that."

"He has a troublemaker of an ex."

"Excuse me?"

"You heard what I said."

"Fuck's sake, honey. Just giving you a heads up."

"And why would I need that from you?"

"Right. Thomas is just the greatest. I mean, he's brilliant. But he has hangups."

"So do we all."

"Yeah. God I love him. He was my first. We were each other's. Him and me, we had our run. Always fun to reconnect when I come back through, just like old times. But he's just a bit mad, that one. Unpredictable, like. His drama will always come first. You'll be off soon enough. But you took care of my ma. So I'm returning the favor."

"I was happy to take care of your mother today. But Tom isn't mad, and I don't need any favors from the likes of you."

"Fair enough."

I lifted my bag onto my shoulder and walked out. I rejoined Sam at the bar. Tom handed Declan a rack of glasses. Susan's heels clicked past behind me.

"You all right?" Sam asked.

"Don't know."

"Thomas! Come say hello, will ya? You don't mind, do you, Frances?"

Susan plopped down beside a couple in the corner and beckoned to Tom with a theatrical wave.

"Tom," the man in the corner hollered from across the pub. "Ah sure, come here."

"Be right back," Tom said, and slid in beside Susan across from the couple.

"Jesus, Mary, and Joseph," Sam laughed, looking between me and Declan as he wiped the corners of his eyes. "The manky mouth on that one."

"She just accosted me in the bathroom. What's going on?"

"Sadly, I cannot explain, Frannie," Sam said. "Declan, talk some sense into your brother, will you?"

"What did she say?"

"Tried to 'warn' me about Tom. Said he slept around."

"Fecking slag," Declan muttered.

"Don't listen to that cow," Sam said. "I'm the prize around here."

"Not hungry, Frances?" Declan asked.

"Lost my appetite. Is this a regular occurrence?"

"No. She hasn't been back in ages."

"I'm about to trigger the smoke alarm," Declan said. "One more?" he asked Sam, and Sam nodded.

"The fuck?" Declan said. He was staring behind me. I followed his gaze and saw Susan press herself up against Tom, their faces inches apart. Then she closed her lips over his. Tom was motionless, his back to us. She'd laid a manicured hand on his neck.

"For fuck's sake," Sam said.

Tom turned to the bar. He caught my eye, said something to Susan.

Declan stared.

"What an absolute cunt," Sam said. "I'll kill him."

Tom appeared to one side of us.

"What the right hell is the matter with you, you prick?" Declan said.

"Frannie," Tom said.

I pushed my chair back and stood. Susan leaned against the pub door, an unlit cigarette in her mouth.

"I can explain," Tom said.

"Sam," I said.

"Fran, don't go," Tom said.

"No need for chatting, Tommy," Sam said. "Let the lady go."

Tom tried to move past him, and Sam pressed his finger into Tom's chest.

"Let me explain. She'd give that to anyone."

"And she most certainly did. To half the fecking island."

I pulled my bag onto my shoulder and walked into Maude's darkened store. I walked outside and across the street. I'd never noticed until this moment that the town lacked streetlights. I fumbled with my keys.

Inside, I looked at my dad, the box that used to be a body, a beating heart.

One time, the vehicle driven by a twenty-nine-year-old man had collided with a semi, and then he was unresponsive in the ICU. His family stood around him as he died. I gave him his last bath before wheeling him down to be extubated to prepare for organ donation.

"Sometimes I can't stand this fucking place," the charge nurse said and left.

"You okay?" Indira asked.

"It's been three years. I'm still not used to it."

I glanced at the picture of his wife beside his bed. We stared at the motionless body before us.

"Remember, once we pass through to the other side, we're no longer able to distinguish ourselves from others. He's about to be reunited with an ocean. He'll never be alone."

"His wife will."

"His wife is not your patient."

She walked away in her squeaky shoes.

Was my father a drop in the cosmos? The little box of what was left of him looked so small on the little Formica table. He was the one I wanted to give my love to. Who else would take my love? Who would bury me?

A cardboard box was no place to spend eternity.

I took the Archer sweater off and tossed it on the dresser. I knelt before the fireplace. I stacked the wood as I'd learned. I struck the match, dropped the flame in, and waited. Firelight flickered against the cottage walls.

The phone buzzed with a text message from Brigid.

Thanks 4 2day

Happy I could help. You good?

Yes! See you tomorrow 😊

The next one was from Declan.

Dont mind the tart 🙈

Tommy didnt see that comin

I'm going to bed 🖤

I opened Instagram, logged out of Brigid's daughter's account, and punched in my own username and password. I searched for "Thomas Archer." Nothing. "Tommy Archer." Nothing. I searched for "Susan O'Brien," but too many came up. I narrowed the search by geographic region. I scrolled through a long list until I saw one with a Snapchat filter adding glistening features. "@susieQQQ." Not private. There was one of her in a crop top in front of the Eiffel Tower. Another on Oxford Street. Another in Amsterdam. Her posts for the last few months included pictures with a dark-haired man who looked like he'd been forced to pose. Then, dated about a year ago, a photo of Susan perched on Tom's lap, his arm around her waist, his sunburned smile. People commented, "sooo cute," or "you two are ADORable." I logged off then plugged the phone back in. Brigid had insisted I keep it on me at all times.

26

...

That night I choked on the stench of whiskey as Anton, his scalp garlanded with a crimson ribbon, squeezed Toby's windpipe shut. I gasped, sat up, and counted my breaths. I put the kettle on and watched a patch of fog float among the boats. Tom had invaded the night, and I was a traitor who'd invited him into my tranquil land. I'd forced the moment and brought us too close, too fast, though there'd been indications, for a woman with eyes to see, that it wasn't time.

I heard steps on the path, then three knocks. Three more.

"Fran, open up. Gotta let me in, Fran. I heard the kettle. I know you're in there."

I opened the door to a view of Tom's face.

"Frannie, c'mere to me."

"I'm tired, Tom. It's been a long one."

"Can we talk?"

"Not in the mood."

I pushed the door. He blocked it from closing and slid a shoulder through.

"What are you hiding from?"

"Here I stand in plain sight."

"Please talk to me."

I opened the door. Tom stormed in and walked to the hearth.

"Did you light this?"

"What do you want?"

"Are you alone?"

"Until a moment ago."

"Sam stormed off. You two looked pretty close in the pub."

"You think I'm shagging Sam."

"I don't know what to think."

"Let's see. He can't be hiding in the dresser, unless I chopped him into pieces. If I'd stuffed him up the chimney, he'd have suffocated, and the place would be full of smoke. That leaves the tub. But we should also check under the bed, just in case."

"What happened tonight?"

"Ask your ex. The woman is a regular hall of records. Cat got your tongue? Okay then. Why did you come to her family's house with me?"

"I don't know. In case anyone needed help."

"In case anyone needed help that you would provide, using your extensive training and long experience in healthcare."

"I guess I was worried she would be there."

"Is that so? Fine. Let's say it's true. We're all there. Frannie is there. Susan is there. And then, what a relief, Tom is there. Now what? You're going to do what, exactly?"

"Prevent her from running her fecking mouth, maybe."

"You didn't do much to prevent that in the pub. Except kiss her."

"I didn't provoke that."

"Did you know she was going to be in town?"

"No idea. I can tell you're upset."

"Yes, I am. You could have talked to me instead of tagging along. And afterwards you're all over her. After I'd spent the day taking care of her mother."

"I was not all over her."

"Your mouth was. And then she looks at me like she knows what she's about. How embarrassing."

"I'm embarrassed too."

"So why kiss her? Why in front of me?"

"She kissed me. She did it. Felim was right there. Shocked him too. It didn't mean a thing."

"I had just spent the night on your boat. Everyone saw me leave that next morning. And then you're kissing her."

"What should I have done?"

"I'd like to be alone."

I opened the door and stood aside as the cold air entered.

He pushed it shut.

A man's hands could hold you above the waves or grope his ex or choke your brother or knock your mother down.

"I didn't go to her, Frannie."

A log in the fireplace cracked.

"Do you really hook up with American tourists who come through Inis Mór?"

"I don't run around chasing girls on holiday."

"Susan told me you enjoy 'getting to know' the tourists passing through. She said I should watch out."

"Now that's a load of bollocks."

"So you don't sleep with the American tourists?"

"I've met a few girls. What does that matter?"

"Americans?"

"One was Canadian. I'm just being honest. You don't regret any of the men you've been with?"

"I don't date with a mindset of planned obsolescence. And I haven't slept my way through the tourists, anyplace I lived."

"Jesus Christ. It wasn't all of them."

"I hope you were careful."

"I've been careful. Do you test your partners?"

"I do, actually. We both test."

"Before a shag."

"Before a shag. Don't you think about those things?"

"Not always."

"Do you care if you fuck a bully? Because I don't fuck bullies."

"What does this have to do with anything?"

"Tonight I found out you have a bit of a reputation."

"You listened to that shite?"

"She followed me to the bathroom, right before you had a snog in the corner."

I hadn't thought this through. In my attempt to shield my past from him, I had neglected to inquire about his. The poster child for working-class Ireland was a player, and I was just another girl.

"You think I just sleep around."

"I didn't say that. Susan did."

"You never had a hookup."

None of my bedmates had been strangers. But there had also never been anything beyond the acrobatics of lovemaking. "Is that a problem?"

"How did you meet men then?"

"I don't know. At work. At the library."

"The library."

"Not much craic there, I suppose."

"Sorry I don't spend every afternoon prospecting in the reference section."

"It's not the pub."

"That was a long time ago."

"Yes, from a certain perspective, tonight was a long time ago. For instance if someone knocks on your door in the wee small hours of the morning."

"I don't know why she went on about all that."

"To hurt you. She said it to hurt you."

"Frannie, you aren't a hookup. You can trust me on that. Tonight was a fecking mess, but relationships get that way."

"That's where we differ. I don't put my mouth on an ex when I'm in a relationship."

"Do you think I would put the moves on her right in front of you?"

"I think we rushed into this."

"Because of Susan? I couldn't give a shite about that cow. She ambushed me. Everyone saw. For fuck's sake, this is not something I rushed."

"I don't want any entanglements. I have a nice life here. I'm tired. Tomorrow I have to catch up at the clinic."

"Stop pushing me away. I know you're tired of running."

"What I want is to talk tomorrow."

"I'm not leaving."

"Please go!"

"Jesus Christ."

"I'm not falling for a guy with bad boundaries. Or someone who doesn't leave when you tell him to."

I walked to the door and opened it.

"Not a problem. Clearly you don't know me at all."

He left, shoulders slumped.

Michael Collins peeked out from behind the rocking chair, looked at me, then at the door, then at me, and scampered off.

27

...

The clock on Wanda's mantle ticked. The windows rattled. I locked the door and rubbed my face. This wasn't how it was supposed to happen. I'd been wrong to think it would be different this time. He was damaged, I was scared. Why risk it? I took two ibuprofens, lay in bed, and stared at the ceiling.

One semester I worked on the Neuro floor of our hospital, where I performed frequent assessments, such as cranial nerve tests, for patients who'd suffered traumatic spinal cord injuries. A man in physical therapy described paralysis to me as "a heavy nothingness." He directed his legs to move, and they didn't respond. He performed the exercises, and no matter what he commanded his muscles to do, they wouldn't move.

I shut my eyes and opened them on Kilmurvey Beach, where I stood in tall grass and watched the skeletons of drowned fishermen limp ashore. I asked their names, but no sound came out of my mouth.

A little wraith, ankle-deep, waterlogged, took shape among the big ones, with light eyes and a pale face, like Tom's but smaller, long strands of wet black hair matted against his forehead. I recognized him. It was Seán.

Then a dark blur shimmered far off. I squinted and walked across the sand to get a closer look. This was my father, appearing the way I'd drawn him since his death, but as if a cartoon artist had animated my sketch, so that it strode weightlessly through the surf. My father told Seán, who'd advanced ashore further than the rest, to come back out to the shelf where they were hovering. Neither saw me. I shouted, "You're not there," but the dream swallowed my voice. I waved my arms, signaling to the shades that the only person who saw them was asleep.

My dad turned to me. Where my pencil lines had been, I now saw a young man from a Polaroid. It was as if no time had passed, and I was a kid, but at the same time, it was like staring into my own face. I spoke, and a sound I'd forgotten came back to me, as my father's voice issued from my lips. "Take me home, Frances," I said.

I sat up in bed. I looked at his box. I cried. I was bereft as always, in a cold room in a foreign country, with embers in a fireplace.

What home?

28

...

I dismissed the mirror and rubbed my swollen eyes. Pain pierced my brain. Fatigue wore out my limbs. I coughed and combed my hair. I was coming down with something for sure.

The last shoelace, the last shave, the last coffee in the favorite cup are unknown as such to the person who dies, but the one who lives looks back at these things—along with the last time falling asleep together, the last time splitting a pretzel, the last time quarreling, anything at all associated with the deceased person—and sees them not only as themselves but also as final memories from "before," and soon discovers that this altered perception changes the details of life "after" into meaningful facts as well, freshly vivid and yet to be known, albeit postlapsarian and bereft of simplicity. In view of death, the world of the living is made new.

The babysitter looked at the clock and sighed. The phone rang. From the rug I saw her lift the receiver from its cradle. She turned away. I was hungry. She said my mom was busy at work and couldn't talk now, but I was allowed to keep watching TV.

Mom climbed into bed next to me.

"You up? There was an accident, honey. Frances?"

I almost felt relieved that something had happened to confirm my hunch. The car had broken down, or a nail had gone through his hand.

She said she'd been to the hospital.

After that, I lay awake and listened to the nightly silence supplant nocturnal parental sounds, voices over shows, the next day's lunch being prepared. I would think of that first night, on the afternoon, years later, when my mom disconnected our landline.

It was the birth of fear.

Now I saw myself getting dressed for a departure, not so much to a place as from it, let's say my mother's house or my college dorm or my nursing school apartment or the United States.

For years I'd made do with very little, so strongly had I felt the urge to decamp, a spare heap of items kept close, easily packed. The pixelated, grainy photo Mom had sent the week before showed the two of them at Toby's basketball tournament. He'd grown tall. They were fine.

The imperative to take him home, which he'd delivered to me through my own voice in a dream, was neither command nor plea, but both at once.

For the ancients, the manner of burial determined the character of rest. I wondered whether Dad's soul had been confined to the Bardo, and languished there, shoved in a closet as Mom slept next to another man, thousands of miles from his family, his hunting dogs in Sligo, the old churches next to their property, the vestibules he'd stand in before the start of Sunday Mass.

I'd brought him within a few hundred miles. Lingering too long. Had he been adrift as I was? Impatient?

I crept past the pub with my pack on and walked my bike the long way around Fishermen's Row. Both Archer boats were gone from their slips. I pedaled up to the clinic.

I dreamt the day away, replaying the night before, thinking of the things I should have said, completing my tasks by rote. I forgot my patients and had to look up their charts when Brigid arrived.

I was glad things hadn't gone further with Tom. His flirtation with Susan would have hurt if we'd had sex.

Summer wasn't over yet, so there was still time for me to screw up some more. How stupid to fall for a jilted man who told me he'd just gotten the ring back. Anyone could end up together, even Susan and Tom. I saw his arm around her waist, her sneer, and the kiss, a set piece of the head trip I'd been on. Stupid to think I could matter to him so soon. I savored my self-pity.

Brigid came in. She said she had to make a house call and asked if I'd be all right on my own for a few hours. I said yes and sneezed.

"I'll be back in a bit then."

"Sure. Would it be all right if I took a day or two off?"

"Everything okay?"

"I'd like to see Sligo, where my father was from."

"Are you taking his ashes?"

"Yes, though I don't feel ready."

"Even if he's gone, he's still your da."

I tried to unscrew the ibuprofen bottle cap.

"Eight is too young to lose a father. You all right?"

"Headache. I feel closer to him than to my mom."

"Any fever?"

"I haven't been sleeping."

"Of course you can have time off. Might it be that you need a break from town as well? Don't act surprised. Word travels fast. People talk. And the O'Brien girl is wicked, that one."

"Tom doesn't seem to think so."

Brigid pointed her thermometer at my forehead. "One hundred point four. Let me see your throat. Anyway, Tommy can be a pleaser. Has been since they lost Seán. No trouble, keep everyone happy, don't rock the boat."

"Is that why they're all so protective?"

"You noticed. We can't have Maude lose another boy. Especially since Tommy thinks Seán's death was his fault."

"I wish I'd known he and Susan were still involved."

"Before you fell for him?"

"They kissed. Right in front of me. In front of everyone."

"Don't you bother about that girl. She casts a wide net. No need to go swimming into it. She's been causing trouble around here since she was small. Tommy proposed to her. She accepted, then moved on to other blokes, including friends of his, starting drama with the wives, before he'd even caught on, they were quits. Her family was ashamed. We were all delighted when she moved away. Tom would be smart to steer clear."

"Why is she trying to get his attention if she didn't want him the first time around?"

"I don't know. People like her don't care much for themselves, but they sure wish others did. It's a curious measure of a person's worth. Love on the installment plan."

"When she kissed him, he just sat there. Made me feel like a fool."

"You're not."

"I don't know what I was thinking, falling for a local guy."

"What's wrong with that so?"

"It's not what I came here for."

"Why did you come?"

"I'm running from my life. My family, my dead stepfather, my hometown, the people who knew me, gossip, cruelty. I want to be an old Aran lady hanging her laundry and rubbing her sore hip."

"There's cruelty everywhere, Fran. Even on our little island here."

"I don't need anyone."

"That's no way to go about. You can let your guard down around good people. You know the difference. Don't close yourself off. You'll forfeit the good things, too. Ní hé lá na gaoithe lá na scolb."

"What?"

"'A windy day is not the day for thatching.' It's like a verse out of Ecclesiastes. All things in their season. Bide your time. Are you in touch with anyone in Sligo?"

"Dad's people are long gone."

"Hotel?"

"Not yet. I plan to wing it. Mom said before he died my dad's people were good to her, the time she came over."

"Sligo is lovely. A friend owns a pub there. I'll give him a ring and tell him you'll be by."

She handed me an address she'd scribbled on the notepad.

"Mom always said my dad wanted to raise us there, but she said no."

"How come?"

"Too unfamiliar, maybe. I've been putting this off. I have his ashes still. I've been carrying them around with me since I was a kid."

"Hard to let go."

"You'll be okay on your own for a few?"

"You've worked nearly every day for the three months I've had you. I'll be back by early afternoon, and you can catch the evening ferry to Galway. Go see your da off. And give that Tom a bit of time to come to his senses."

"Thanks, Brigid."

"Body aches?"

I nodded.

"That script is for Oseltamivir. Text me if you start feeling worse."

"See you next week."

I booked a ticket on the Aran Island Ferries. After a one-hour layover in Galway, I'd take the last train to Sligo. Now I had to get back to my room, pack, and depart without running into any of the Archers, who were at the docks, in the pub, on the roads, all over the place. I had an hour before I'd have to board the boat, so I took the long road to Dún Dúchathair, where there were fewer tourists and I could focus on my father's dream words.

"Take me home," he'd said.

Seabirds circled above the waves. I walked along the cliffs. The tourists cycled off, and I got close to the edge to look at the limestone far below, and saw two men sitting beside a small fire, a bundle of sticks beside them.

I arrived at Wanda's in the early afternoon and parked my bike on the north end to avoid the pub's patrons. The phone vibrated with a call from Declan, and I heard a few taps on the door. He was aproned and disheveled, and he held a paper bag in his hand.

"You've been avoiding me."

"Not you. The rest of the world."

"Save me from that pub. An American couple complained for twenty minutes that our Camembert grilled cheese sandwich cost sixteen quid. 'That's higher than London. How about half?' Can you fecking believe? You look awful."

"Thanks. Come in."

"Are you sick?"

"Maybe."

"Are you contagious? Should I get a mask?"

"Most of my symptoms are existential."

"Contagious."

"To what do I owe this visit?"

"Did you get my text?"

"I did, but Tom's mad at me. I didn't know if I should respond."

"He is mad at you."

"We fought."

"For fuck's sake. What a shite day."

"Once I asked an ICU doc how his day was going, and he said, 'Better than my patients' days.'"

He pushed the paper bag across the table.

"I brought you a salad. Maude said you hadn't been in. She's up to ninety on account of last night. Not speaking to Tom."

"Sorry."

"It's that dryshite tart who should be sorry."

The water boiled.

"Got anything stronger?"

"Fanta?"

"Perfect. I have to talk to you about something, and then I have to get back before ma's left with the orders piling up." He took his glasses off, sighed, and rubbed his eyes.

I poured tepid Fanta into two glasses and sat across from him. He watched the dockies lashing boats to their slips. His features were Tom's, but finer.

"Tommy said he's told you about our Seán."

"He did, yes. I'm sorry, Declan."

"And about him being in the hospital?"

I nodded.

"He was almost a goner, you know."

"We all have a past."

"Last night gave you a peek into Tom. It wasn't him at his best. He was weak, and I told him so. Sam and I both did. After you left. It was a bad scene. Very Donnybrook. Tom moved to go after you, but Sam lit into him. Pushed him back. Twice. Almost decked him. Tom can be petulant, but he's no match for Sam's right hook. I had to get in between them. Shouting and all. Sammy got in a good shove before Tom left in a huff. I don't care for violence in any form, but I work in a pub, and I can break up a scuffle. Anyway, Maude wanted me to come talk to you."

He paused, looked hard at me, and said, "She's scared you're going to up and leave him. Susan always brought the sour with her, but this isn't about Susan. When we were growing up, in our teens, Seán just a wee guy, Tom was a man about town. Confident, smart. He was going to take over our da's business. Tough but kindhearted. All our da's hopes pinned on him, and he didn't cave. Tommy, he looked out for all of us. But me the most. I wasn't out, but people could tell I wasn't straight as soon as they heard me speak. There were more than a few times when he gave someone a talking to, or a proper beating, for hassling me."

"He stood up for you."

"Your boyfriend resorted to violence."

"No one should have picked on you."

"Tom has put a few blokes in headlocks for talking shite. But the worst came from none other than Susan."

"Worst of what?"

"Running her mouth."

"What about?"

"Me being 'a queer,' she'd call it. One day after a few too many she told me I was choosing a manky life of sin. She'd shagged half the island. She'd be picking and choosing her sin there so."

"I've met her, and I believe that."

"I blew it off. Not the first time I'd heard a load of nonsense. Tom and Susan had only been dating a short time when I left for Paul Bocuse, so I didn't think of it."

"Sounds fancy."

"It was brilliant. Met someone there as I told youse, and after I came back, he came through Ireland for a visit. Still does from time to time."

"That reminds me, I met a friend of yours."

"Uh oh."

"Flight nurse from Galway."

"Straight, unfortunately. Just a friend. Anyway, Daniel from Lyon. Gorgeous man. Tall as Hozier, never misses a day at the gym. He was in Maude's when Tom came in for a pint, Susan with him. Daniel got into it with Susan about Brexit, and she called him a faggot. Right there in front of Tom, in front of Maude. She said, 'What would you know about it, you thick faggot?' I was in the back with the dinner, or else I'd have thrown her out myself. Tom stood up and lifted her by the arm like, and walked her to the door. Told her to see herself home, he'd talk to her later. They were engaged by then. They'd met with the priest twice. The pub was packed. Everyone in town. I'm shocked it wasn't in the paper the next day. Daniel was cool. Not like we hadn't heard that sort of thing before. But Tommy broke it off with her, as you know."

"That was the reason why?"

"I was feckin' delighted. Tom took it hard. Whole thing made him quiet. He gets that way when he's thinking, kind of shuts down."

"I saw a bit of that last night. She said nasty things about him."

"Like what?"

"Called him crazy. Told me to watch out."

"Did you tell him she said that?"

"No."

"Rough row?"

"He stormed out."

"Do you want to know what happened next?"

I nodded.

"She kept texting him, saying the drink made her say it, and she was sorry. Tom talked to me first, then our parents. He didn't know what to do. Man was lost like. On the back foot. We knew he was fond of her, but hoped he wouldn't take her back. We wanted him to be with someone who didn't have the cruel in her. Sometimes we settle for a spot of warmth where we can get it, though."

I'd tried, but I couldn't have sex without fancying that I was in love. I couldn't abstract my emotions from sex, but I didn't want to be starved for love either. I thought I could withdraw from the need for love and control my desire, but that didn't work out, since I still felt it, so I tried to distract myself with nursing and drawing and listened to other women discuss the conflicts and delights of husbands and boyfriends. Love was something they experienced. Not me. Until Tom. Everything was different with him. I'd told my secrets, touched him, been touched by him. There was no way to be on your guard with a man like Tom.

"I feel so out of it today. I'm thinking about life before Tom. Love before Tom."

"And how was that?"

"Unremarkable."

"Care to elaborate?"

"You were telling me."

"You know about our brother. Tommy took losing Seán the hardest. A part of him went away. The whole business was feckin' awful. I thought I was going to be an only child there for a bit. Long story short, Tom told Susan he needed time to think. Spent it on his boat, out on the water by himself. It was good for him. He came back ready to talk with her, at least. Meanwhile, though, and keep this between us, that wagon consoled herself by shagging a stone mason who came up with Tom in school. Tom didn't know. Sammy talked about it one night in the pub, thinking he knew. Tom said she wouldn't have. I don't know if he was back with her already, but he called her right then and there, from the kitchen in the pub. She said nothing happened, they'd got together for a few drinks. But she and this bloke had spent a night in a hotel room. I don't think you need a paid room away from your own house to watch football. Sam suggested Tom go to the mainland to clear his head. He stayed with old friends from uni. Came back after a few days. Susan moved to London soon after, and she was going around with someone new in no time."

He shifted in his seat and said, "My point in all this, Frances, is that he hasn't been the same since. You need to know my brother might be in love with you. He looks happier than I've seen him since Seán. Healthier. He looks like he used to be before. But I think he's not over the fact that he lost two of the people he has been closest to, his brother and his fiancée. He freezes up when faced with the possibility of being deserted. He's a good man. The best I know. I don't want him to end like Cúchulainn. He froze up last night, but he's good to the core."

"Thanks. But that kiss spooked me."

"Girl, me too."

He noticed my bag on the bed.

"Are you leaving?"

"Why can't your brother talk to me like you do?"

"Please."

"I'll be back in a few days."

"Sligo, then?"

"Don't tell Tom. I just need some time."

He leaned forward and took my hands in his.

"If you two love each other, you'll have the most loyal man in the world."

A foghorn announced the ferry's arrival.

Declan hugged me and left. I wrote a note to Wanda saying I'd bring chocolate for the kids, and asked her to please tell Maude I'd be back in a few days.

I packed the salad, a few clothes, cash, my sketchbook, and my father.

WILLIAM BUTLER WHITE
DOB 9-25-68 DIED 12-12-02

I pocketed Brigid's loaner phone and peered out Wanda's front door. Tom was talking through the pub window with Maude, who stood with hands on hips, firelight in back of her. When a group of tourists passed, I joined them and split off to board the *Saoirse na Farraige* down at the docks, lights flickering in the fog.

I sat near the back window and watched the yellow glow from Maude's pub shine on the island through shrouds of mist until, with our eastward progress, it dimmed and disappeared.

29

...

A few townsfolk rode the ferry, including a patient Toby's age, whose mother had been scowling at us ever since Brigid prescribed the minipill to treat her periods, and who waved and smiled with a mouthful of braces, surrounded by friends, when she saw me. I waved back. The captain dimmed the lights.

Anton and Mom went down the street for dinner a few weeks after Toby was born, and left me to watch him. As they stepped out, Mom told me to call if the baby woke up.

"Don't worry!"

I sat by the crib with my sketchbook. He slept on his belly. Large pajamas, little fists. I watched him breathe. I touched his hand. He held my finger. My leg fell asleep. I kept still.

The night Anton attacked my little brother was the only time he and I ever talked about what had happened. He came into my hospital room. The social worker stood in the doorway. I sat on the chair next to the bed. The doctor had given me a list of directions, which I held in my lap, but wasn't allowed to read.

"Hey," he said.

"Hey."

"You okay?"

"I'm okay. How are you feeling, bud? Come here."

I patted the seat next to me. He sat, and I held him. He was stiff in my arms.

"What are those?"

"Paperwork."

"You have a concussion?"

"I see them all the time at work. Not serious."

"Frances?"

"Yeah?"

"Thanks."

We sat like that for a while.

Toby deserved doting parents, a father to teach him to shake hands, throw a football, tie a tie. Those things were out of reach now. I'd taken them.

Then I left too.

The ferry docked at the Galway port with a jerk. I disembarked and walked toward the train station. The route led me through a crowd swarming the city center. Some nights the pubs on Inis Mór closed before the sun had set, the last patrons shuffling home by nine o'clock, but last call in Galway was still a ways off. Bright shops lined the streets, and queues stretched past buskers, where people blew on cups of tea and sipped pints. Muffled beats thumped through nightclub windows. A slurry of discourse flowed from open pub doors. Local bohos handed flyers to passersby on the cobbles. I walked through the city and pasted its image over those of the night prior. I crossed a River Corrib footbridge far from the crowd and sat facing west, the direction I'd come from. Friends and couples lounged, legs dangling over the indifferent swans. Two gulls lit on a bit of wrapper and indulged in a dispute. I sketched a couple down the pier who sat back-to-back and passed a joint.

"Hey, that's good," said a boy Toby's age, easel under his arm.

"Thanks. What have you got?"

"Watercolors. Tourists love them. You can make a few quid if you sketch over on Quay Street."

At the train station, bag against my chest, I thought for sure your face had been there among the faces in that throng, pickpocket. You could be almost anyone. Under the station lights I leaned on a bulletin board full of ads for rooms to rent and bands. I hadn't slept in two days, and a cold ache gripped me. Symptoms indicated I was heartsick with the flu.

I took a seat in the back of an unoccupied train car and watched the ticket taker advance down the aisle. We moved noisily north. The conductor dimmed the overheads. I closed my eyes against the past few days. Craggy Salthill and bleak Burren sped by. I woke as sunrise warmed the grimy window and we arrived at MacDiarmada Station in my father's birthplace.

Beyond the slate gray of the station arose a mantle of rough green. I shivered with the chills. A sparse crowd walked the streets my father had walked in his youth. I headed south toward the town, past some surfers, boards fastened to an old RV for a trip to Mullaghmore. In the distance I saw Ben Bulbin over a row of buildings in the morning sun.

I stopped for coffee in a corner café. A woman led a troop of children wearing navy blue uniforms, holding hands. A man across the street played a pipe next to a poster for a Sofas show. I followed the directions to my lodgings. Brigid had told me to ask for Glen at Connolly's Pub. He'd lent me a room for the weekend. His brother had gone to medical school with her, and she'd called to tell him I was coming, so I'd get a fair rate. I entered through a heavy door and sat at the bar next to two men drinking milky tea over newspapers. Another played a guitar in the corner. The bartender nodded.

"I'm looking for Glen. My name's Frances."

We shook hands.

"Brigid's friend. You'd like a room."

"Yes. Through Sunday."

"No trouble at all. I have one with a view of the Wild Atlantic Way, and one with a town view."

"Town view would be great."

"I'll take you over in a bit. What'll you have?"

"Coffee."

The men looked up over their papers.

"Make it Barry's."

Glen nodded.

I looked around. A sign read 'ESTABLISHED IN 1866.' Caps, metal boxes, crucifixes, crisps, and sweets lay stacked on display. A man in the corner, a pack of cigarettes on the table in front of him, sang a song about how Dublin kept on changing and nothing seemed the same as before.

Glen served my tea with a hunk of brown sugar and a cup of milk, then returned to his register and counted stacks of tickets from guest check pads like the ones we'd had at the Dublin pub.

"This place looks like something out of history."

"Well over a hundred fifty years old. It was my father's before it was mine. I've tried not to change anything."

"Is that a phone booth?"

"Ah, that's the snug," one of the men said. "That's where the women would have to go to drink before things were equal, so they say."

"Now it's a relic from the old days," Glen said. "Poor lassies would pile in there, sometimes ten at once. Times past were good times."

"Aye," the man said. "What's new is good, though sometimes I wish things could stay the way they are forever."

"Can't tell the future, sure we can't," Glen said.

I sipped the tea and flipped through the guidebook. I wondered whether, as the singer had sung and the old man had said, the best times were over and done, and all that I or anyone else could expect was to put one foot down in the future and keep the other in the past, one on the pier, the other on the deck of a vessel going out to sea. I opened my sketchbook to my father's Polaroid. '*Billy & Molly, 1982.*' A boy dressed in plaid with a pipe in his mouth and a speckled hunting dog by his side in front of a sagging two-story house, the family farm indistinct in the background. I wondered whether the building was still there and how far away it was. I'd never thought to check.

He would have turned fifty-six this year. His parents went a few months after him. Mom said they died brokenhearted from losing their only son.

I stared at my father's face.

The photo was stuck to the back of the Archer postcard. I peeled them apart and set the postcard down next to my tea.

"Could I have a pint, please?"

"With your tea?"

"I think so, yes."

"Are you sightseeing in Sligo today?"

"Not today. I have some difficult business."

The old men looked up.

"No trouble, I presume?" one said.

"She's a nurse, for Christ's sake, Kevin," Glen said. "You're not planning on getting yourself into any trouble, are you?"

"No trouble. I'm here for a funeral."

"Ah, sorry ta hear it," Kevin said.

"In that case I recommend a whiskey. Won't slow you down as much as a pint."

"I've never had whiskey."

"I'm a Diet Coke man myself," the man next to Kevin said.

"Americans like Jameson," Glen suggested.

"Don't feel so American these days."

"I like Bushmills," Kevin said. "On me."

"No trouble at all," Glen said.

"I'm Kevin," Kevin said. "This here's Alastair."

"I'm Frances," I said.

We all shook hands.

Glen poured a glass each for me and Kevin, neat, then a finger for himself and a Diet Coke for Alastair.

"Cheers then?"

The four of us drank, the men tapping their empties on the bar. My throat burned.

"Mind me asking whose funeral you're attending?" Glen asked.

The soft gaze of heavy eyes. A man's frame, with the face of a boy.

"My dad's."

I showed them the photo.

"Ah, I'm sorry, love," Kevin said.

"He was born here. Near Ballincurry. This is him on his family's farm."

"I don't know the fellow," Glen said, handing the photograph to Kevin and Alastair.

"Hundreds of farms here in Sligo," Alastair said.

"Not as many as Cork, though," Kevin said.

Alastair rolled his eyes. "Southerners."

"So where's the funeral? Immaculate Conception?"

Glen returned the photo.

"I have his ashes. My plan is to scatter him next to who he was named after."

"Who was that?"

"Yeats."

"Ah, Drumcliffe," Alastair said. "Me ma's buried there. I'll be too, God willing."

"May God rest his soul," Alastair said. He raised his glass.

Glen poured another for the rest of us.

"To William, then."

"To Dad."

30

...

I took the only open seat, on the aisle next to a dark-haired boy Toby's age who wore a soot-stained sweater and carried a chicken under his arm. I held my backpack on my lap to keep my dad close for our final trip. When I'd packed my bag that morning in the rented room, with its view of a narrow street and no sea, I'd thought of this journey as a picnic of death.

Looking at the silent green landscape, I reflected that my dad was the only person in my life who never let me down. He didn't live long enough to leave a scar, aside from his death, which hurt me everywhere and nowhere at once.

After Anton died, the court, which hadn't found me guilty, mandated therapy, so I met with a social worker named Vicki once a week for six months. I didn't have much to say at first. She had a tabletop Zen garden with grey stones and a wooden rake you could use to comb grooves into the sand. The way she looked at me made me think she thought I was a psychopath, which is how I thought everyone else in town perceived me. After a few sessions I asked if I was her Pavlovian dog. She laughed.

"What are you afraid will happen?"

"He'll come back and get me."

"Even though he's dead?"

"I know he's dead. But in my dreams, I don't wake up in time to save Toby."

"We process in our sleep what we can't face awake."

"What if there are others like him?"

"What if there are?"

"I can't tell the difference. What if I let the wrong one in? How can you tell?"

"You can't."

"So what do you do?"

"You take a chance or you don't."

The bus pulled over, and the brakes hissed.

"Drumcliffe," the driver said.

I sidled up to the front.

"How much time do you want?" he asked, an open magazine on his lap.

"An hour, please."

"Grand."

I stood on the shoulder as the bus lurched away, tires crunching against the gravel, and watched until it disappeared. Drumcliffe, next to the highway, was empty.

I walked around the side of the church, where a small graveyard sat, by hill after green hill, and a herd of sheep.

The church door was locked.

One o'clock.

I wondered what time of day my dad was born, more than fifty years ago. I thought of Toby as a baby, knuckles wet in his mouth as he teethed.

I stepped between stones and found Yeats' grave alongside the pathway, grey and unimposing.

```
Cast a cold eye,
On life, on death,
Horseman, pass by!
```

I dropped my bag and took out Tom's book, whose cover had gotten creased and worn. I opened to "Under Ben Bulben," the poem Yeats wrote about his approaching death. The fortress Ben Bulben, the site of a legendary standoff between the Republic and the Northern Irish, hovered in mist at the low end of the graveyard. My father would have seen this same view growing up. I reread the lines "Many times man lives and dies / Between his two eternities" and asked myself how I had "died." My dad's death. When Anton went after Toby. In Maude's pub the other night. How was I going to live safely, and not die, between my two eternities?

The weight of melancholy lifted, and I thought clearly about these two fathers, the one who'd died too young and the other dangerous one, clearly and without agony for the first time. I'd never viewed what I did to Anton as an effort to defend my family. He had it coming after what he did. Tom called me a soldier that night on the boat. I'd done what was right—not that doing right doesn't cause pain.

I was ready. I had no business speaking to Anton's spirit, but sitting there in that old graveyard, I slowly inhaled and breathed out a cold goodbye, and let him go.

I'd always thought of death as the absence of life. If life was force and the body's response to force, then death was a lack thereof. Unresponsiveness. No breathing. No reflexes. No pulse. One day, a doctor will lean over, shine a light into the eyes, and look for a reaction. Death is when there isn't one. The moment we die, a transfer occurs. Our bodies go to work. Flaccidity takes over in our muscles, skin, and fascia. Next is pallor mortis. Blood recedes from the top layers of skin, causing the body to cool and stiffen.

Death comes for those we love, those we fear, and those to whom we are nothing.

I cut the box open with my pocketknife and lifted my dad's ashes from the sealed cardboard. I'd never looked inside. His remains were in a plastic bag. A life reduced to a few handfuls of greyish dust.

I placed the bag on the grass.

"Thank you for keeping me company for as long as you did. I've brought you home, as you wished."

I scattered the ashes.

They fluttered on the grass, shone in the sun, sifted onto the earth, and flashed in a gust of wind that picked up and dispersed them in a brief whirl.

I told Vicki about my dreams of Anton's face and hands, and the pool of blood. I told her I couldn't sleep, and the night shift distracted me.

"You lived through a traumatic event. Of course it's on your mind. You can't help that. But you can control how you react. Close your eyes. Sit back. Where's the fear?"

"I can see his face in my head."

"Not the source of the fear, but where the fear is."

"My heart."

"Picture the heart. Tell me what you see."

"It's red."

"You're a nurse. Tell me."

I described the heart.

"What would you say to soothe your heart? Not medically, but as if your heart could hear the words you said."

I closed my eyes. In my head I held a human heart in my hands. It beat—or, as I thought when I first saw one during emergency surgery, throbbed—too fast. I listened to Toby's heart with my stethoscope in nursing school. Then the CAGBs at the hospital, the patient anesthetized. I recalled another patient who walked out of the hospital four days after open-heart surgery. Tommy's heartbeat when he and I first kissed. Mine when we first touched.

"What would you say?"

"What I said to my newborn baby brother: 'Shh, I've got you.'"

"What else?"

"I'd tell it, it was safe."

"What would your heart do?"

"Slow down."

"If the choice presented itself again, would you cause harm to prevent harm?"

"Yes."

The bus pulled over. At the sound of its brakes I looked up and saw faces behind the windows. The driver opened the doors, and I broke into a run, but before I could round the church, the wheels crunched on the gravel, and the coach pulled onto the highway.

Church, bell tower, graveyard, sheep, clouds.

Pickpocket, the little Aran island had become a home, a place I was needed, where I'd fallen for Tommy, and found peace.

I stood beside Drumcliffe Road, shivering, feverish. I picked up my bag, lighter now, climbed to the shoulder, and walked.

It began to rain.

I stuck out my thumb for an oncoming truck, old, exhaust in its wake. It pulled up past me, a faded rusty Bedford flatbed with wood slats fencing a load of hay. As I approached, several full-sized pigs, lounging in the back, lifted their snouts and sniffed the air.

A man with a white beard, his face sagging with age under a porkpie hat, smiled through the open window. The orange upholstery of his bench seat was stained brown by smoke from the pipe in his teeth.

"Need a lift?"

"Guess so."

"Where ya headin'?"

"Main drag."

"All right then."

He held a piglet in his lap.

"That's a little pig."

"She'd get trampled in the back. The bus driver leave youse?"

"He did."

"Come on then. Haven't got all day."

I opened the door and climbed in. He shifted into gear.

"He leaves tourists at least once a week. Do you know how many people sit on the side of this highway, stranded so? Seatbelt, please."

"Sorry. I've never seen one so small in real life."

"You can hold her if you want. Most piglets don't like to be held, but I start to handle them so after they're born. Helps with temperament and all."

I lifted the piglet. She squirmed like a puppy, nuzzled my sweater, and wagged her tail.

"I appreciate you stopping. Hitchhiking can be risky in America. I was hoping you weren't a murderer."

"Pig farmer."

"I'm Frances."

"My name's Gabriel."

Pipe smoke filled the cab.

"Like the angel."

"Suppose so."

"What's her name?"

"This one is named Ma'am."

"She's the size of a newborn baby."

"She's two weeks today."

Gabriel talked all the way to town. He asked about my work, then told me about his aching hips, his wife's hips, the pigs' hips. I told him his symptoms were consistent with arthritis and recommended some activity modification. He protested that he was as strong as ever, and attributed his good health to good genes and good whiskey. He insisted he'd take me to Connolly's, instead of dropping me at the train station where I'd boarded the bus. He and Connolly Senior were in school together, he said.

"Third grade. Scoil Phadraig Naofa. He was a dope then. Reckon he's got his act together now."

He craned his neck to look in the steamy pub windows. Across the street in the dance studio on the second story, little girls lined up at the barre. I handed wiggly Ma'am back to the Archangel Gabriel, said thank you and goodbye, and stepped out into the rain.

Connolly's was packed. Glen stood on a chair and slapped the side of a mounted television. A few men watched, hope in their eyes and pints in their hands.

"Howsagoin', Frances! Pint?"

"Tea, please."

A large family entered, and he removed empty glasses from the bar.

"How did it go?"

Glen walked back and forth among patrons, some of whom turned to listen. I told him.

"She took her father's ashes," Glen said.

"Ah, that's lovely," a woman said.

"Me gran had chickens on our farm," another woman said. "She rocked them to sleep in her arms like babies."

"That driver forgets people all the time," Glen said.

"Thank God for Gabriel," a man said. "Our Uber."

"Cheers for that," Glen said.

"It was the most dangerous thing I've ever done," I said.

"This isn't America," Glen said.

"I've seen every season of *The Sopranos*," the first woman said. "Nothing like that here."

Glen set down a cup of something steamy with cloves and sliced lemon.

"Hot toddy?"

"For your throat."

Two tourists in wetsuits. Men with sooty boots on, back from work. Middle-aged women sitting over pints. Young men loosening their ties, watching the game. I sketched Gabriel in the margins of the guidebook.

"Need help with that map, miss?"

It was Tom.

"What are you doing here?"

"This seat taken?"

He dropped his sack and sat.

"Nice place."

"What's going on?"

"I heard you weren't feeling well."

He opened his bag and took out a scarf.

"You came eight hours to bring me this?"

"Five hours, yeah."

He lifted my hair and wrapped the scarf around my neck.

"Old fisherman's remedy."

"How'd you know?"

"Birdie told me."

"Birdie?"

"Population seven hundred forty-two."

I sipped my drink.

"I came to apologize for Susan. I shouldn't have let her touch me. I messed up. I've been in bits thinking about things. She caught me off guard, and I froze. But I did a shite job. If I'd ignored her, nothing bad would have happened, but I didn't, and it sent the wrong message. I feel like an eejit for not seeing it from your perspective. I'm horrified she ran her mouth about my past. I may have had some wild years, but I don't sleep around."

"The women in town said she did that on purpose when she found out you were seeing someone."

"Yeah, they told me that too, a few hours after you snuck off like a thief. Sam lit into her. Called her a tramp."

"Pint?" Glen asked Tom.

"Aye."

"Probably good you left when you did. Susan came to the bar for a drink. Sammy asked her where the craic was, that she was barely in it for once. That set her off, and she started running her mouth, which she seems to do with a bit of drink in her. Then Sam called her a huair and she had a go at him. He stopped her hand so. Then Wanda and Maude got in front of her, telling her it was best she moved on for the night. Ma had to call the Gardaí."

"I didn't know there was a Garda station."

"Remember Colin from the pub? He was at the clinic too when Sam busted his face. He's the guard."

"Your uncle is the cops."

"Station's behind his house. Anyway, Wanda dragged Susan out, all hollering like. Sammy called her a right embarrassment to the island. Colin cited her for public intoxication. But Fran, I should have spoken up."

"Why didn't you?"

"I think in my head by not saying anything I was hoping it would all go away. But more importantly, I'm sorry I didn't leave when you asked me to."

"I'm sorry I pushed you away."

"Was today your trip to Drumcliffe?"

"This afternoon."

"How did it go?"

"I said goodbye."

"Declan told me to let you be, but I was scared I'd lose you. Can you take me there for a visit?"

"Okay. But only if we rent a car. The bus driver left me stranded. I hitched a ride back with a pig farmer."

"Nice of him to give you a lift then."

"I made it in one piece. What are the odds?"

"Agh, that family is older than mine," Glen said.

"This isn't America," Tom said.

"Are you eating tonight?" Glen said.

I reached for a menu. Tom put his hand on mine.

"Frannie. Look at this."

Tom reached inside his jacket and took out the postcard, my postcard, his postcard, and placed it on the bar.

"Where'd you get that?" I asked.

"It was under your whiskey when you left for Drumcliffe, and I kept it here on the bar, and Tom came in and saw," Glen said.

"Where'd *you* get it?" Tom said.

"It was in a book."

"Where?"

"Dublin."

"Whose book?"

"Yours. Or it used to be yours. When you were in school in Galway. I guess you sold it back to the bookstore."

"How'd you find it?"

"A busboy at the pub where I worked needed help with a paper. He had a Yeats book, and this was in it."

"Is that the same one you tote around with you?"

I nodded.

"I can't believe it."

"Yeah. Must have sat tucked in there for years."

"When did you figure out I was the one from the postcard?"

"Right away. As soon as Maude sold me the sweater."

"Why didn't you mention it?"

"What would you have thought if I'd told you I followed a postcard that happened to be yours?"

"I'd have thought it was brilliant."

"I was in the back, between shifts, with noise all around, and people and bustle, and the image felt like it came from another world, and that attracted me, I guess."

"Fran, it's fate."

"I don't believe in fate."

"I need to tell you something."

"Okay."

Here we go, I thought. He slept with Susan on Fisherman's Row. Or aboard his boat. Wherever.

"I looked in your sketchbook. Remember that first night when you left your bag at Maude's? I had to. We didn't know whose it was. I felt like I was watching you sleep or something. Maude told me to return it to you. But then she looked over my shoulder and we both saw that you'd drawn me looking out the side of the boat. You caught me thinking. That's my favorite part of the day. Sailing back home. When I can just be there with the waves and the gulls. I don't care if it's only been a few months. Don't you see what's right in front of you? Christ. I didn't come all this way to apologize. When I saw that picture you drew, I thought maybe I had a chance. But you were this elegant girl. I figured someone like you would prefer a fella who didn't have to wash his hands at the end of the day."

"I have to wash my hands. I could get staph."

"When we're together, I feel like you get me, you see me for who I am. You know I don't make much money. You know I was in the hospital. The postcard feels like a sign. All day on the water I look forward to seeing you. I wonder if you'll be sitting on your stool at the bar when I get there."

"And I'm the one who keeps her cards close."

"You couldn't tell? When we went swimming? The night on Da's boat?"

"I hoped."

"I almost told you sooner. People have gotten married in two weeks here. I want to keep you safe. I want you in every way. But I was scared you think I run a fishing boat and don't have much to offer."

"Did I give you that impression?"

"No, but I've pinned my hopes on the wrong ones before, and got burned. Then I was left with the same pair of boots and a mother who told me to sturdy my heart till the right one comes along."

"People can do what they want, but the way I see it, if someone's going to let you touch their body, they should let you touch their heart."

"Remember when you asked me if I'd always stay on Inis Mór? I can't bear to lose the pier, the place where Seán last walked. I want to stay where he stood."

"I wouldn't leave either."

"I love you. I'd follow you across all of Ireland. Across the world. Where do you want to go?"

"I don't want to go anywhere. I want to stay with you here."

"This pub?"

"This country."

"We're all right then? I didn't ruin my chance at something lovely?"

I embraced him and nodded. He held me in his arms. I kissed him. In front of everyone.

Glen placed two shot glasses in front of us and poured whiskey into each.

"Who got married after two weeks?"

"Two weeks after a blind date."

"A blind date on Inis Mór?"

"It has been known to happen."

"But who?"

"The Reagens."

"It can't be a blind date if you're cousins."

"Not true. That was a lie, industriously circulated by their neighbor, whose land they encroached upon, admittedly."

I laughed and wished we were alone.

31

...

I got what I wished for.

I have you, pickpocket, to thank for it.

I had to make him make love to me. Men like Tom don't push. I put his hand on my hip, and he looked in my eyes to make sure. The difference was, his people understood I loved him, and I wasn't going to hurt him. Years later, we would talk about how, even before our first night together, after the swim or the quiet moment by the hearth, we'd each thought, not without fear, that perhaps the other could give us a child.

I felt lighter, as if I were in another world, where the edges of things were soft, and I took Tom's hand and strolled with him down Abbey Street as dusk stained the River Garavogue amber and aubergine.

"Painter's Hour."

"You're burning up."

"I'm okay."

The pub's sounds faded, and we walked past darkened shops to the rented room with its view of the street. I dropped the keys in a puddle. He used the light on his phone to find the matches and tilted his head to check the flue. He squatted at the fireplace. I sat on the bed. Light crackled in. He sat beside me.

I placed my hands on my knees. He kissed me.

"You're shivering! It'll warm up in a minute. Should we give Brigid a call?"

"I'm fine."

"You're not sick from me stressing you?"

"It's viral."

"Maybe we should get you to bed."

"I haven't gone to bed with anyone for a while."

"Same here."

"How long?"

"Last year. You?"

"Since the States."

"No one seduced you in any of Ireland's public libraries?"

"I checked the catalog under F, for Fisherman, comma Poet, but all the copies were loaned out."

"I was sure Sam stole you. He's in love."

"You can't fall for someone who has access to your full medical history."

"Since it's your favorite spot for prospecting, do you know how many libraries there are in this country? I looked it up after our row."

"How many?"

I laid a hand on his thigh, and the muscle tensed up.

"Three hundred and thirty. Think of the women I could have met!"

"Since we're on the subject, I got tested after my last partner."

"You can't do that yourself?"

"Run my own bloodwork? At the lab in my rented room?"

"I did that too. On account of the dodgy ex. Irish Family Planning, here in Galway. Perfect marks."

"Good man."

"Listen to the Yank, talking like one of us."

I leaned back. Tom sat by the fire and unlaced his boots, his suspenders dangling. He stood and handed me a crumpled paper bag. I opened it and found a box of condoms and a candy wrapper.

"I wanted to be prepared this time."

"I didn't figure you for a Cadbury man."

"What's your favorite?"

"Guess."

"Turkish Delight?"

I shook my head.

"Toffos?"

"Nope."

"Tell me."

"Chocolate oranges."

He stood in front of me. I looked up at him. I reached for his waist and parted my legs.

I lifted his shirt and kissed his abdomen, the muscles firm and silvery in the low light. He shuddered, drew a sharp breath, and looked down, lips parted, gaze soft. I felt for his heart.

He lifted me and laid me down.

Astride my hips, face above mine, he brought his tongue to my neck, tracing my collarbone, my mouth.

"I'm contagious."

"Don't care."

His mouth moved from my neck to my shoulders. His hand slid from my ankle to my knee, then higher. His lips brushed my breasts. I ran my thumb against the line between his eyebrows. I lifted myself beneath him. I felt my wetness and heat.

I'd studied the human body for years. How could my cells regenerate, but not my emotional life? In phagocytosis, white blood cell membranes engulf the bacteria responsible for infection. I would have liked to hunt down and destroy anything that exposed me to distress, but I'd locked myself inside the past, and now it was time to make an effort, even if it put me in harm's way. How could I ever love someone if I also didn't leave myself open to being loved, and therefore hurt, by them? I pictured a stone fence. I walked in among its guard dogs, entered a gate, and searched for Tom.

I kissed his brow, his eyes. He gripped my sweater. I pulled him along me, breathing his scent. I moved my lips to his neck. I stood and removed the sweater. I took off my jeans and tank top. He got down on his knees and caressed my thighs, brought my chest to his mouth, inhaling at my sternum. His callouses felt rough.

I climbed on top. He touched my face, and I pressed my lips to his palm. His hands swept across my shoulders, my breasts. I tasted him like that first night on the boat. I lifted his sweater off and ran my hands over the muscles of his shoulders, the birthmark on his chest. He cupped my breasts in his hands. I moved my mouth to his chest, his abdomen. He rolled me to my back, his hand under my waist. He moved his mouth to my nipples, lower, my belly, he slid off the rest of my clothes, hands on my buttocks, kissing my thighs.

"I want you," I said.

I wrapped my legs around his waist.

At first we went slow, then fast, his arms tight around me.

It felt the way it was supposed to feel.

After, breathless, he lay with his face in my hair, our legs entangled.

"Remember the seisiún?"

"Feels like a long time ago."

"Everything's different now."

"Being in love changes the way things look."

"I won't let anything come between us again."

We slept. I felt him stir against me and looked at him, naked in the grey predawn.

"Tell me we'll be together."

"We will."

We woke. He got up and tended to the fire. I coughed.

"Take these."

"Tamiflu! Brigid asked where was I."

"I pressured her."

"You came all this way."

"You don't have a phone, but I'm crazy about you, and therefore I'm prone to feats of courage."

"Is that how that works!"

"Don't question science. You're brilliant. Exactly as you are. Tell me something I don't know."

"I'm a killer."

"There has to be something else."

"I'm left-handed."

"Are you left-handed so? In my life I have never met a single left-handed person. You might be a cailleach."

"It's possible. I'm going to brew a potion."

"What kind?"

"Ex Repellant."

"About time you Americans did something useful. Make a batch. We'll douse the whole of Ireland."

"Your turn."

"I once sailed through a hurricane. Third or fourth time out on the trawler, we ran into bad waters, ten-, fifteen-foot waves. We were all of us thrown about. Sailed right through. Fantastic. Safer than on land actually. Nothing to smash into. The best was when we'd be standing on deck and the bow would hit a wave. Some nights I'd go up and listen to the sea, and later I'd lie in my bunk and hear the sounds of other ships through the hull, a lullaby."

"What about when it wasn't storming?"

"If the seas were warm and we were alone, we'd have a swim. 'Hands to bathe' is an announcement that means it's time to dive. Captains would pipe it over the ship's tannoy. Kind of an all-hands-on-deck thing, but to knock off, ease up on the throttle, cut the motors. We'd jump twenty feet from the freeboard. The nets would drop for us to climb back up. There'd be fifteen blokes jumping in."

"I'm going to have to share you with the water."

"You can be my first mate."

"I love you."

"Mo ghrá thú."

"What's that?"

"'You are my love.'"

"This morning you're having tea. With honey."

"Thank you, handsome."

"You don't mind if my shoulders are uneven? My right one is an inch shorter, from carrying everything on that side."

"I don't mind."

He put on his coat, reached into the pocket, and handed me a folded a piece of paper.

"I wrote this after Inis Oírr."

Then he went out.

I got up and spotted his red hat in the sparse crowd, then read his handwriting on the lined sheet.

Fran

Some things unsaid
are best up close,
names of lines, the end
a love or friend left
behind us that lists
what we'll have time for
if the wait lasts
and what hasn't been
becomes a first
last line drawn out,
we wish, ever ending.

Tonight I try less
to clear my head
of your murmur,
soft against tarnished
breath on a mirror,
hinting at a name
I got from dreams,
and think to admit
now you know

how often I revisit
the way from any angle
you stare into me
at no one, and say
what I wanted to.

The light brightened and cooled beyond a bend in the street as the sun climbed. Men in work boots walked past, and children tugged on their parents' hands.

The human heart circulates six quarts of blood every minute, pumps between eighteen hundred and twenty-two hundred gallons of blood per day, and beats one hundred thousand times daily and between two and three billion times in a lifetime.

I looked up and saw Tom a block away, cap over his ears, two cups in his hands, a bag under his arm.

32

...

On the boat ride back from Sligo to Inis Mór, I stayed close and watched him steer through the port and navigate out of the shallows into darker seas. I felt his weight, love like a pressed flower, the taste of a bruise.

We refueled in Galway. I disembarked and bought him a cup of black tea from the station café. Then I stopped at the terminal ticket booth, beside a crowd set to queue up and board the Aran Islands Ferry. I tapped the glass in front of a young clerk who futzed with his console under the fluorescent glare.

"I have a return ticket from Inis Mór to Galway that I don't need, in case someone else does. Last name White, first name Frances. Here. Have a good one. Thanks."

"If you don't mind waiting, miss, just a moment, miss? Miss!"

"I know it's not refundable, you can comp someone."

"You left these last time, I believe."

The man with the cigar rummaged in a locker, opened the door next to the window, and handed me a plastic bag.

Inside were my purse, cell phone, passport, and apartment key.

Tommy untied his boat. In the captain's chamber I plugged in the phone and watched messages and notifications cram the screen.

I pulled it from the charger and switched it off. Tom started the engine, and I opened Brigid's loaner phone and positioned the camera to catch the two of us. I texted the image to Declan, then Brigid:

On our way home

In the photo, I stand with my arm around Tom's chest. He leans
toward me at the wheel, lips against my temple, the mainland
behind.

Acknowledgements

Thank you to JackLeg Press, especially editor Erik Noonan.

"An Cailleach" imitates a poem of the same name by Brigid Dolan, a school librarian who writes poetry and fiction.

"Fran" imitates a poem entitled "Some Subjects" by Steven D. Schroeder, whose latest book is *Wikipedia Apocalyptica.*

"Stockholm Syndrome" imitates a poem of the same name by Dillon Wilfong, a carpenter and musician living in St. Louis.

I relied on my daughters, Dr. Taylor Ramsaroop and Camille Cundiff, R.N., to answer myriad questions about the medical professions, and I'm grateful to them for their help. Thanks also to Dr. Bill Bowman, who taught me about the human cardiovascular system. And thanks to Dr. Daniel Hammer, who explained the half-life of DNA in bone.

I'm grateful to Lieutenant Mark Portwood of the Royal Navy, who showed me how a fisherman views the land and sea. May he always find a warm fire to sit by at the end of his day.

Thanks to those in Maynooth who welcomed me into their home before I'd made one for myself, and to Gabriel, of Sligo, who gave me a lift at Drumcliffe Cemetery.

Thank you to my husband, Chris Reed, whose editorial eye answers to his heart.

JackLeg Press Authors

jacklegpress.org

V. Joshua Adams
Mark Baumgartner
Gayle Brandeis
Scott Shibuya Brown
Michael Chin
Chloe Clark
Rivka Clifton
Brittney Corrigan
Jessica Cuello
Barbara Cully
Allison Cundiff
Curious Theatre Branch
Neil de la Flor
Genevieve DeGuzman
Suzanne Frischkorn
Victoria Garza
Reginald Gibbons
Joachim Glage
Caroline Goodwin
Brett Hanley
Summer Hart
Kathryn Kruse

Brigitte Lewis
Jenny Magnus
DK McCutchen
Jean McGarry
Rita Mookerjee
Mamie Morgan
Beau O'Reilly
Lex Orgera
Zach Powers
Karen Rigby
Jo Salas
Maureen Seaton
Kristine Snodgrass
Cornelia Spelman
Peter Stenson
Melissa Studdard
Jennifer Tseng
Gemini Wahhaj
Megan Weiler
David Welch
Cassandra Whitaker
David Wesley Williams

JACKLEG PRESS